LET ME LOOK AT YOU

LET ME LOOK AT YOU

MICHAEL J. WILSON

KINDRED BOOKS
GREEN BAY, WISCONSIN

Published in the United States by Kindred Books, an imprint of Brain Mill Press.

Print ISBN 978-1-948559-49-2
EPUB ISBN 978-1-948559-52-2

www.brainmillpress.com

This book is dedicated to the "schoolmasters of ever afterward."

"Do not hide your face from me, for I would gladly meet my death to see it, since not to see it would be death indeed."

—Augustine, *The Confessions*

LET ME
LOOK
AT YOU

Chapter One

CONTESSA BECAME A FIXTURE IN MY MIND A YEAR AGO WHEN I SAW HER BOARD THE TRAIN. She found a seat near me and started reading a book by Paul Laurence Dunbar—I couldn't make out the title. As the train carried us out of Brooklyn, I watched as she read from the middle of the book. At about three o'clock, she caught my glance and smiled. I wanted to walk over and say something to her, but in the next moment she left the train. She looked back at me and said, "Bye, Adrian." She knew my name, and I didn't know hers. The thought both frightened and fascinated me. From that day forward, she became my obsession.

Before then, my love life was uneventful. I had spent passionless hours in front of the TV or seated at the dinner table with women whom I'd met through friends. But Contessa (a name I invented for her because of the noble way she entered the train and sat directly across from me) bore the promise of endless fascination; she was the first woman who came to me as a stranger. Our eyes met accidentally.

I should say now that I am not moved merely by the looks of a woman. I happen to know that beauty without intellect is an impressive ship lost in a fog. Unable to plot a course for itself, it cuts through the ocean at the discretion of the waves, never certain if it will see the harbor or stay plunged in darkness forever, the grandness of its construction rendered useless.

So when I make initial contact with a woman, the first thing I take into account is not so much her face, but her expression. Is there any light there? Is there softness? Or has her light been extinguished, her visage resigned to dullness and moodiness? Contessa had a beautiful face, to be sure, but it was her countenance that subdued me. We only made eye contact twice; she looked up at me first. Although I said nothing to her, I knew that we had initiated a little game; we were starting a kind of dance where one has to stoke all the cravings of love from afar. If this little scrimmage is performed successfully, then the more aggressive forms of courtship can be slowly introduced.

She walked onto that late afternoon train in Brooklyn and sat across from me wearing a turquoise, loose-knit sweater that revealed her collarbone. She wore a pair of light blue jeans tucked snuggly into brown boots. A knit cap matching her sweater sat on her head, half-revealing an unruly hairstyle. All of this was made more dramatic by her red lipstick, which gave her the look of a young girl trying to look more adult, mature and slightly jaded.

Her intelligence was radiant; she owned a set of high cheekbones infused with enough warmth to retain the softness of her features. Her outfit and makeup were far from remarkable. Jeans on a woman have a way of dampening my lust, but judging from the brief moment when I saw her saunter onto the train I knew that she belonged in elegant robes. She struck me as a descendent of the Egyptians, fully able to trace her lineage back to the nineteenth dynasty, propelled forward in time yet sworn to secrecy in order to move about New York without causing a stir. Nevertheless, I was affected.

That same day, when I got home, I looked online to read the horoscope for Virgo. I wanted to know if it said anything about finding a new love. It didn't. When horoscopes match reality, we say that the stars are truly powerful and hold a mystical control over human affairs. When they don't, we dismiss them as senseless. Of course, I could not be deterred so easily. I began plotting the next day's encounter. It was during that planning phase that I came up with the name "Contessa." I estimated that it was about twenty minutes after three o'clock when she boarded a Manhattan-bound train at Atlantic. She made her escape from me at Fourteenth. Where was she going? She had no excess bags, so she couldn't have been shopping. She was traveling alone. She didn't seem to be dressed for a job. Was she just visiting New York for the day? That would have been horrible, and I consoled myself with the thought that, as it was fall, she was probably a student. But how could I be certain? There was only one way to know for sure, and it involved taking the same train at the same time the very next day.

In preparation, I went about putting together a perfect ensemble in which I would make the grandest impression on Contessa so that she would not hesitate to give me her real name. Approaching a woman on the street is a delicate affair; one must be careful not to startle her at any point during the confrontation. The man should look well-kept and be smartly dressed. He should be confident yet graceful. To obtain the little victory of exchanging numbers, he should time his approach so that it seems unthinkable to the woman to let the moment vanish without a sequel. The first impression, that moment when I step out of the tapestry of city life and become a single, vivid person to her, must be handled with the greatest care. I must deliver myself up as mysterious but not secretive, ready for the sexual act but not searching for it that evening. She will make up her mind in a matter of seconds; if she gets on well with me then I can enter the next phase. If I am blown off, more care is necessary to get her to see just what it is she has tried to disregard.

My attire would be the first thing she would notice if she were to see me from afar. A man's closet should be limited to just a few high-quality and versatile pieces. I'm thinking of the white collared shirt, the leather jacket, the sport coat: the look of an urban professional. For Contessa, I chose a leather jacket and a white shirt paired with dark blue jeans, black dress shoes, and a gold watch that would expose itself only when I extended my arm to hug her. I ironed the shirt and hung it on the closet door. The jeans I kept folded and the watch I placed near my cologne and deodorant, all to be worn the next day. With these particulars in order, I sat in a chair opposite my bed and began thinking of ways to establish contact with Contessa. I only had a small amount of information to go on. She was about five foot four. She was not a snazzy dresser—at least not during the week—and she wore her hair in the natural style, which could have meant that she lived in Brooklyn, like me. Perhaps she went to school along the 3 train. Maybe she was a photography student. But then, where was her camera? She could have been on her way to a poetry reading. "That was it!" I thought—she must be a poet. Why else would she have Brooklyn hair and a noble expression? It would do me some good, then, to brush up on some of the famous poets who weren't men. I had not touched them since college because most of the modern ones struck me as too feminist, wary and leery of men like me. This is why I gave my admiration to the earlier women, like Hurston and Grimke. I thumbed through my old copy of the Norton anthology and found the works of Phyllis Wheatley, whom I held in the highest regard. Wheatley commands a certain respect among lovers of verse even though her oeuvre is perhaps the least known among the greats. To quote a few lines of her work to the would-be black poetess of today is to take control of the game altogether.

Just the same, I would be amiss if my intentions were to flaunt information unknown to my prey. One must inject a bit of flattery into a conversation about poetry. Every girl wants to believe she has some in-depth understanding of spoken word or the verse of Gwendolyn Brooks, but to ensure that my flattery is aimed perfectly, I like to quote the works of our timeless singers like Lauryn Hill and Erykah Badu whenever I'm asked, "Who are some of your favorite poets?" They don't bother over the little things like nails and cars, and they see in love the union of souls, not a mere business arrangement.

There was a possibility that Contessa might not be a poet. One brief encounter on a crowded subway car was not enough to be sure. It would be better to simply throw myself to the wind and seek her out on the subway the next day. Ordinarily, I would have smoked a small cigar and watched videos online just before bed, but I decided against my routine. I needed my face to be as bright as possible for the next day. The tobacco would have dried me out and made my face too pale to make my approach successful. At 9:30 p.m., I turned out my lamp, turned the radio volume down to a whisper, and promptly went to bed.

It was fifteen minutes to three, and if I walked quickly, I could be at the 3 train platform in time to catch Contessa as she boarded. I weaved through a circus of tourists, beggars, performers, and wanderers. A construction worker who was walking with his head down as he swiped away at his phone bumped into me. He didn't even acknowledge me. There was no use saying anything to him; I couldn't risk a scene that might make me late for my rendezvous. Besides, it was a fight that I most certainly would have lost. Just looking at his burly knuckles and ripped jeans reassured me that an altercation would have meant my downfall. I wiped the thought from my mind and forgave him. Walking farther along, my path was blocked by a stream of tourists flowing up from a lower level. There must have been fifty of them, perhaps a dozen or more families. The fathers cradled cameras and wore closed-toe sandals with Old Navy fleece; the mothers donned capris and fanny packs; and the children—still reeling from the thrill of their train ride—wore miniaturized versions of their parents' clothes. Some of the smaller kids looked at me like a curiosity. I grinned, believing it to be the appropriate counter to their innocence, but I was also embarrassed.

The children looked spotless against the backdrop of underground New York. One could almost have called them *uncontaminated*—like those little pristine cherubs in Renaissance paintings—were it not for their goofy socks, popsicle-stained fingers, and general air of confusion as they argued over which train would take them to the Statue of Liberty. The group finally decided on a direction, and the foot traffic in the station filled in the space they had left behind when I heard someone yell out my old college nickname. "Addy B!" I shivered.

The only people who shortened my name from "Adrian Bellinger" to "Addy B." were friends from school.

It was a well-intentioned way for them to show they liked someone, butchering a person's name like that. It would have been taken as rude if I had kept correcting them, so I let it slide, though it always secretly annoyed me. But to hear that name yelled out in a crowded subway station, as if I were at the heart of some scandal, was the very height of embarrassment. I turned toward the voice. It was none other than Marcelle Lockett, my former roommate who had been expelled sophomore year for selling weed out of the dorms. He was from California, and this was the first time I had seen him since he popped up at a nightclub during my senior year of college. He had arrived clean-cut, well-dressed, and with drugs to sell. He immediately became the center of attention. There was no sign that he'd been fazed by the break in his education; in fact, he looked better than he did when he was a student. Marcelle was a flashy dresser. He had arrived at that party wearing a blue, trim-fit Versace suit. By the end of the night, he had managed to persuade two girls to sit in a lounge chair with him in the back of the club. By then, he was only wearing his pants.

Now, in the train station, he waded through the crowd toward me with outstretched arms. The sight made me smile, a real smile.

"You in New York too now?" and he gripped my hand to pull me in for a hug. Marcelle was younger than me but had the confidence of an older brother.

"Well, how long you been up here for?"

"Like eight months," I said shyly. I didn't want to sound like a *new* New Yorker.

"Damn, man. I got here last week. I love it up here!"

I was relieved. "You got a place yet?"

"Nah, I'm crashing on—you know Jessica Walton? I'm staying on her couch until I find something."

Jessica Walton lived in Bed-Stuy, three blocks up from me. "Does she still stay on Monroe?"

"Yep. Crazy thing is, I'm not even fucking. I'm trying to move up out of there before I do, though; she's not even my type."

What Marcel meant by type had everything to do with Jessica's looks, but she was only unattractive to me because she couldn't hold a conversation to save her life. She was one of those quiet, only-say-one-word-when-spoken-to types. Not for me. As for Marcelle, his good looks had not faded. He was smart and still handsome, with a courageous face boasting high cheekbones and a deep black complexion. He wore a plain white V-neck shirt with a black ball cap turned backward. His silver watch sagged on his wrist and traveled halfway down to the elbow whenever he lifted his skinny tattooed arm. I'd never taken the time to look closely at his tattoos, but I was able to make out some Aztec symbols and a sperm whale traveling along the side of his bicep.

"You still on Facebook?" he asked, pulling out his phone.

Time was running out. I had to get to the platform. The conversation had to end quickly but politely. Marcelle was a good person to know.

"I am, but just take my number and text me for now, I'm already late for this train…"

He understood. "Cool, go head and type it in."

He looked admiringly at the contact information I had entered as if it were the final piece to a puzzle. "Cool, I'm gone hit you tonight, I'm throwing a party."

"Really? Where?"

"Jessica's," he said with a hint of mischief.

We shook hands again and went in separate directions. My water bottle was empty, and I'd started to sweat. I had no choice but to jog to make up for lost time. I thought I would turn a corner and bump right into Contessa, knocking her down, at once succeeding and failing to make a lasting impression on her.

I reached the platform for the 3 train at 3:02 p.m. The timer read "2 MINUTES" before the next train would arrive. Slowly, I scanned the platform like a hawk. Every black woman in sight was analyzed and compared to the image of Contessa I held in my memory. No sign of her. There were two women standing a small distance away, both wearing natural hair in the style of Contessa, but their faces were so foreign, so drastically *unlike* my lover's, that I thought the gods were playing a miserable joke on me. I wanted to walk up to both of them and tell them they were a source of confusion and misery and that they should leave altogether. Before I could, the 3 hissed into the station, spewed out a set of riders and sucked up another, then rattled back into the tunnels. She was still nowhere in sight. Either Contessa hadn't come or the Midwestern family and Marcelle had caused me to miss her. I had failed. At 3:37 p.m., I walked back to the A and took it home.

Chapter Two

WHEN I CAME UP FROM THE TRAIN STATION IN BROOKLYN, IT WAS RAINING. A BROKEN umbrella had landed upside down in a puddle in the middle of the street. Its curved handle was jutting out, forcing cars to drive around it, and this made for a big traffic jam. When it rains in Brooklyn, whole neighborhoods look war-torn and abandoned. Someone had run into a pole, bending it across the sidewalk. Three trash cans were on their sides spewing garbage. I walked into the door of the frowning brownstone where I kept a room, stomped up the stairs, and flung my wet clothes on my bed. After changing, I noticed I had received a text message. It was from Marcelle:

Addy wuts good. Here's
the info for the party. 650
monroe street. It's the

> homegirl tracy birthday.
> She got BAD friends...
> it's gone pop. Come thru
> nigga!

I threw the phone aside and sat down at my desk. I did not like to receive texts, nor did I like to respond to them.

The text message represents one of the greatest incursions into one's private space. Mail, both traditional and electronic, is satisfied with waiting days to be opened and responded to. The phone call carries with it a note of seriousness, because the caller intends to hold a conversation, and a voiced conversation requires the simultaneous agreement of both parties. If the receiving party does not desire conversation at the time, he or she can simply not answer the call and respectfully divert it to voicemail. But the text message is more invasive. When it is sent, barring the outrageous, the sender knows its contents have been read, if only by virtue of the fact that she can count on a smartphone user to be looking at his phone constantly throughout the day. The text message says of itself, "No matter what you're doing, I know you're going to see me—perhaps immediately." To tell a friend that I didn't see his text invites a wry look, and I become a scumbag in his eyes. Once the message arrives, it's as if a fuse has been lit somewhere; I become obsessed with the proper way to respond, sometimes at the expense of my current obligation. If I send something back immediately, I risk inaccuracy of tone; if I wait

too long, I disappoint the sender. To compound the
matter, my immediate reply is followed by one of two
happenings: either the original sender fails to reply in
a timely manner, thus leaving me feeling cheated; or a
whole battery of texts begin to come my way, pulling
me further and further out of my privacy. And while
the text can potentially deliver welcoming news like,

> Hey, im outside.

> Want me to pick up some
> beer before I get there?

> Free Msg: CHASE Fraud:
> Did you purchase $21.64
> at LubeOil Gas on 3-17-
> 2024. Reply 1 if yes, 2 if
> no. STOP to end msgs or
> HELP

it can just as easily deliver the terrible,

> Are you up? We need to
> talk... its an emergency

> I'm pregnant

> Aye dog, I need to ask you
> a favor. Hit me when you
> get this... ASAP!!!

Texting is often a way of "feeling out" or taking the temperature of someone without agreeing to be subjected to the same kind of examination. Texting is a passive-aggressive nightmare.

"Does Contessa text?" I wondered. It had to be taken for granted that she did—I did, though I was never one to initiate a text conversation. Ours would be a relationship that always used our voices. We might lose sight of each other's feelings and subtle concerns if we chose to type our thoughts to each other too often.

Outside, the rain had stopped, and the sight of sunlight slanting in through my window renewed my resolve to find Contessa. But how was it to be done? At first, I considered suspending my pursuit for a few weeks on the ground that it might be easier to run into a love interest during the summer months, when all of the little flowers come dancing out into the streets, attending festivals and the like. One had only to pick the right concert or fair, attend it, and make oneself visible. Before long, she would come walking right in front of me, just close enough for me to reach out and tap her shoulder. The effort seemed far nobler and more practical than prowling around hot subway stations hoping to spot a girl amid all that confusion. Just the same, summer was still months away, and I wasn't sure which kind of gathering Contessa might attend in the first place. It was after this realization that my eyes turned to the computer screen at my desk and the idea occurred to me that I might be able to find Contessa online.

I felt warm inside and out. I logged into my Facebook and used the filters to view all of my friends living in New York. The results represented a healthy mix; there were graduate students, unemployed artists, native New Yorkers, a couple of old bosses, and, perhaps most important of all, three DJs. Altogether, the list numbered thirty-eight friends. I was willing to wager that at least one of them was a friend of Contessa's. Two hours of searching went by, filled with my looking at pictures of friends and their acquaintances going to the beach, riding horses for the first time, smiling at the Benihana chef's onion volcano, picking flowers, trying out new lipstick, standing on a rock in the Serengeti, drinking from a Starbucks cup, posing under the Manhattan Bridge, walking in the snow, sitting in the window seat on a flight from Philadelphia to Miami, drinking beer, and standing in front of signs—but there was no sign of Contessa anywhere.

My frustration did not get the best of me, though. Often, it is during the darkest hour of despair that the gods stop laughing at the misery of man and throw him a bone. Taking a break from my search, I picked up my phone again to finally respond to Marcelle's text.

"Cool. I'll be there." I sent the message back before I could convince myself not to go. A party thrown by Marcelle couldn't be anything but disastrous in the best sense of the word. When he was still in school, he hosted a party at a house off-campus. He filled the bathtub with an Everclear-based punch and passed out joints to select guests throughout the night. One of the upstairs rooms was off-limits to anyone who didn't smoke marijuana, and there were some people in attendance snorting cocaine in plain view. Toward the end of the night, I remember a couple having discreet sex in an armchair while the rest of the party drank and got higher and danced. There was a certain subset of people who came to Marcelle's parties; they were all drunks, pill poppers, weed fiends, and cokeheads, and they all scored high on their GREs—except for Marcelle, of course.

"My nigga!" he sent back. The words looked funny on my bright screen. Two short words that contained so much volume. In one sense, the phrase meant "my friend," but that was the most superficial meaning. A level lower, and the phrase meant, "You know it's not in your interest to come to one of *my* parties, with you trying to be an upstanding New Yorker schoolboy, but I know that all those hours spent brown-nosing and softening up your 'black side' make it irresistible—and the fact that you can still hear the voice of that little demon inside your soul means you haven't turned into a full blown Tom after all. In short: *Come! It's for your own good…nigga!*"

I hadn't used the word *nigga* for a while, only because I hadn't been around enough black people who used it. I'd never found the word offensive; true, there is the whole history of its abuse, and we all know that every person who was ever lynched was called a *nigger* by some power-drunk, bloodthirsty white man, but I didn't see that as the reason why so many people were upset with *nigga*. The first is, indeed, a racial slur; its metamorphosis is a code word used by the provincial and those who want to maintain some of their provincial spirit. Much the same way *nigger* is disliked because it alludes to the whole ghoulish episode of slavery, rape, and ignorance, *nigga* recalls the ghetto, black-on-black aggression, and a little ignorance as well; people who don't want to be casually reminded of either legacy shy away from both words; those who don't know or don't mind to make the connections use both words at their will. After all, the big crime is that all of these people of African descent are speaking English to begin with; to nitpick certain words in English and treat them as taboo is—for black people—beside the point.

What's up with Tracy? That ur girl, I texted back.

Nope, Tracy Quinn. She
on fb.

Cool

It wouldn't be a bad idea to check Tracy's profile to find out what she and her friends looked like. When I typed "tracy quinn" into the search bar, hers was the first profile to show up. In its miniature form, I could see that there were three girls in the profile picture. She might have been the girl in the middle. All three were brown-skinned. When I enlarged the picture, everything was made clear. Tracy was in fact the middle girl. To her left was a girl who could have been her sister; their smiles were exactly the same, but their eyes were shaped a bit differently. To Tracy's right, standing there smiling right at me, stood Contessa. It made sense that she would have a circle of friends close to my own. How else would she have known my name that day on the train?

When I saw Contessa, I felt rosy. Rosy like a schoolboy receiving that long-sought text message from a crush four seats away in the classroom. A fireworks show erupted behind my eyes; thousands of little streams of light sizzling and scattering between my ears. She was real. There she was: my Contessa, smiling with bright eyes.

Adding even greater delight to my discovery was the fact that her profile was not private. I learned that her name was Simone Regent. I was thankful she didn't have one of those cliché surnames like "Johnson" or "Powell" or, God forbid, "Williams." She had a perfect name to go with her perfect face. She had posted some 756 pictures on her profile, and I looked at each one of them over and over. Now, while I would never have made the mistake of taking her profile to be the whole story, I held to the theory that a person can learn a great deal about another if there are hundreds of photographs to go by. Simone liked the nightlife; she wore short cocktail dresses, she took pictures with a few midlevel celebrities, she danced. There were other pictures of her with an old boyfriend, with her grandmother, pictures with friends from South Carolina (her home state) who all dressed like bammas. This meant that she was like many other girls walking around New York—an *escapee* from the backward, mudbone provinces, hiding behind new hairstyles and new clothes; happy to peel off the rags of their childhoods, only to find themselves adrift in the unforgiving metropolis, oscillating between the desire to appear on billboards or host penthouse parties and the unspeakable thought that they would be better off back home on the farm.

One of her albums, entitled "Senior Year Antics," contained her most captivating picture. The album held about twenty photographs from a house party attended by recent college grads. It was obvious that the house in question was being foreclosed; the walls were covered in chalk and paint and so were the hardwood floors. Back in 2008, people would go to these foreclosure parties and be encouraged by the hosts to trash the place as a way to get back at the bank for trying to sell the home as-is in order to recuperate some of the cost of the failed mortgage.

The picture was framed in such a way as to place Simone in the bottom right corner without diminishing her role as the center of attention. Two other figures, a man and a woman, who looked quite interested in what she was saying, joined her. The male, who was standing at the true center of the picture and to Simone's right, wore a drunken grin and was perhaps standing a little too close to her. The woman, who stood directly in front of Simone, was cut off in the picture; the camera only caught her braids, the dark brown skin of her forehead and ears, and her glasses. She might have been shorter than Simone, but she might also have been sitting. What could be decided for sure: the two women were holding an engaging conversation while the man stood just outside their line of view, waiting for a moment to interrupt. His animated expression fed off the presence of Simone, whom he gawked at as though she were the only woman in the room. To be sure, it didn't appear that the women noticed him, or else they did not want to notice him, even though he was quite close, and their interest and dedication to their topic would not have suffered if the leering man were to suddenly evaporate altogether. A thin layer of sweat coated his forehead, which the camera's flash ricocheted off. If we had seen the same picture magnified and hanging in a gallery, we might first have assumed that he was the subject, but further inspection would have shown that his grin, his arched eyebrows, the very openness of his torso, were all in response to the subtle, natural, and focused beauty of Simone.

At the left side of the frame, just outside the triangle formed by Simone and her immediate audience, another man stood completely out of the conversation, also caught in a moment of drunken admiration. He wore a college sweatshirt and held fast to a can of beer. He was at a perfect distance from the trio—able to hear the conversation and mumble his feelings to himself as he watched. The greedy expression both men wore betrayed them and it was certain that both suitors would have been turned down even if they had gathered the heart to approach her.

There were still more curiosities within the world of the photograph. Another man sat in a chair toward the left side of the picture, in the space between the beer-clutching man and the trio. Although not entirely visible, his posture, his focus on the object in his hand, and his overall detachment from the wider party said that we were looking at one of the first people to develop something I call "chronic smartphone attachment." He had no concern for the beauty of Simone. She was a non-factor to him, but so was every other person in the picture. He sat rigidly in his seat like a man content to exist in a safe, sterile bubble. Checking an email? Sending a text? Looking over a bathroom selfie sent by a lover? We couldn't know. We could only assume that he was an early convert to the life of the phone. 2008: The Year the Phones Took Over.

I was especially attracted to that picture because it was the only one in all of her albums that showed her in candid form; unprepared, unmasked, at ease and natural just as she was during the brief moment when I first laid eyes on her. Her umber flesh revealed its tautness under the flash and showed itself to be of a stronger complexion than all the others in the room. And in conversation, the high intellect in the curve of her profile proved that she must have been of noble lineage. I would have to keep that picture forever. It would either be a consolation if I never saw her in person again, or it would serve as a conversation piece once I finally had her all to myself.

Chapter Three

OF COURSE, THERE WAS NO WAY TO BE SURE THAT SIMONE WOULD ACTUALLY BE AT THE party, yet I reasoned that if she was good friends with Tracy and still in New York, she would have to be there.

I decided to take the relaxed approach. I put on the same outfit that I had been wearing earlier. After freshening up in the bathroom, I sent Marcelle a text telling him I was on my way. He replied immediately, Man, it's wild in here. Come on!

It was still clear outside, though a slight chill had settled in. There were more people out on the streets than I expected. Some were drunk, and some stood in front of stoops listening to music. The haunting glow of street lamps gave the neighborhood a warm quality. At night, without being able to distinguish the color of each building, Bed-Stuy was ominously larger, an infinite stretch of brownstones in every direction. It was useless to look for the "650" on the outside of the building in the darkness. It was as if I were walking through interconnected brick hallways; I would know when I reached the right house only when I heard the right music and saw the right crowd out front.

When I turned onto Monroe, I saw people in a large group farther ahead. As I got closer, I heard laughter. When I was a couple of houses away, I heard Biggie's "One More Chance." People were on the stairs smoking weed and cigarettes or just sitting down to take a break from the heat inside. I didn't see anyone I recognized yet, so I lit my own cigarette after nodding hello to a few people. For a brief moment, the music stopped, and a collective wail could be heard from inside. Someone soared above all the other voices and yelled, "What's wrong, DJ?" followed by the crowd's laughter. Some of the people outside with me took to cupping their hands and looking through the window to see what was happening inside. To my left, a small group had assembled and was discussing some topic with great admiration and passion.

"Of all time? You can't really name an 'all-time' list; it's just so many different styles to compare," one of the men said.

Another guy across from him responded, "Nigga please, greatest of all-time: Big, Pac, Jay, Weezy, Nas— in that order." A few people sighed at this.

"How you put 'Nas' after 'Weezy'?" asked another.

"Nas ain't really have a solid album since *Illmatic*. That nigga is like Lauryn Hill; riding off one good album for like twenty years. 'Least she ain't keep making booty albums like Nas did."

The crowd around him had grown larger. Someone yelled out, "You a fool, Nate!" and everyone laughed.

The first guy, who had argued against all-time lists, spoke up. "We ain't even agree on criteria, my dude. Album sales is different than lyrical skills and so forth. Lyrically, none of them niggas is fucking with Doom."

"Nah, son … Weezy is fucking with Doom, stop it!"

"Who the fuck listen to Doom, though!" shouted an anonymous voice.

Nate started to speak up in a high-flown fashion about the merits of Weezy's style and his overall contribution to hip-hop. The music started again, and so did the party. I left the debate and finally went inside. The party was being thrown on the garden level, so there was a tight squeeze before actually getting inside. It was packed. A single, exposed red light bulb illuminated the scene, and the room was filled with brown shoulders and heads of curly hair. There were cups and empty liquor bottles on the floor. A woman was using her cell phone flashlight to look for a fallen earring. There must have been a hundred people inside. Two women were making out in the hallway leading to the kitchen. When I accidentally bumped into one of them, she gave me an impatient look, grabbed her partner by the hand, and they both disappeared into the living room. I could only move a step at a time; it took me a full ten minutes to get to the bar in the kitchen. Once there, I ordered a rum and Coke and took a spot in the hallway to scan the party for Simone.

No sign of her. I caught sight of Marcelle and walked over to him.

"Wow, man, I didn't know it was going to be like this," I said before taking another sip. I was beginning to sweat.

"Oh, already! All my parties be like this and you ain't even know it," he shot back. Then he leaned in and half-whispered, "You know I got that bud on deck too."

"I'm okay. The drink is just enough."

"All right. Aye! Addy, this is my homegirl Christine. I think she from Virginia just like you." She turned toward me and smiled, then went back to scooping something out of the bottom of her cup with her pinky and sucking on it.

I shook her hand, but there was nothing more for me to say once I learned she was from *southern* Virginia. I'd been down to Portsmouth once, and during a drive to Virginia Beach a friend pointed to a dilapidated shack along the road and told me that the KKK held meetings in it almost weekly. It was the farthest south I'd ever been, and it was far enough for me.

"You don't see nothing you like around here?" he joked. "N.Y. done made you gay and shit now?" He took a swig from the bottle of wine he was holding.

"What? You the one sitting here drinking wine at a house party like a female."

"Whatever, nigga. I *only* drink wine now, got to start slowing down on some grown-man shit."

As he took his lips from the bottle, a group of girls began tugging on his arm asking him to take their picture.

"Hold up, be easy! I'm talking to my boy right now, damn!" he said with a frightening rush of sobriety. The girls left the kitchen altogether.

"What's wrong with you, Addy? You look all worried."

"I'm just looking for somebody, that's all. I'm good, though."

"You sure?"

"Positive. Let me hit the bathroom real quick."

He backed off. I really did need to go, so I squeezed through all of the dancing bodies again and made it to the bathroom line. Two people were in front of me. I debated whether to refill my cup first or hold my ground before things got crucial. I waited. I leaned against the wall and turned the cup nearly upside down to catch the final pieces of ice. When my head was facing forward again, I saw Simone making her way into the kitchen. A loud commotion erupted when she met up with Tracy. I froze. It was really Simone. She looked like she had stepped out of one of her pictures online. She wore a brilliant blue dress with a white flower in her hair. She had even put on a little blush and some of that same red lipstick, too. Her toes were painted soft orange and poked out beneath the bottom of the long dress. I was able to see the full curve of her body now, which was by no means disappointing. I heard the girls in the kitchen calling her over for pictures. She hadn't noticed me, but I had waited too long for that to deter me. I left the bathroom line at once and surfed through the crowd to the kitchen. She was getting a drink by herself while her friends were still taking pictures. It was the closest I had ever come to touching her. I was close enough to catch her scent. She held her cup with grace, but she had the demeanor of someone about to dance in a Southern nightclub without fear of judgment or the anxiety of embarrassing herself. The bartender flirted with her, and I wanted to toss my drink at him for delaying things. She laughed. I stood back a little and waited for the two to finish, but they only grew more immersed in their conversation. She sat her cup down and went fishing around in her purse. A pen! I felt dizzy, I wanted to find Marcelle and make a purchase. The sight of Simone being overtaken by the bartender was unbearable. The fact that he chose to use a pen instead of his phone was an excellent move on his part; having her give him one of her pens was a near coup de grâce. I was forced to retreat. One couldn't follow up such charm without allowing a little time to pass. I stepped aside and turned so that Simone walked past me—even brushing up against me slightly—without seeing my face.

I estimate that a beautiful woman in Brooklyn receives no less than ten advances on an average day, giving us a figure of 140 approaches every two weeks. Of that 140, perhaps two are received warmly. The bartender had stolen one, but the second would certainly be mine. After all, I had something to go on: Simone already knew my name and, what's more, had chosen to call out to me in public. In order to capture the heart of a woman like Simone, a very popular and attractive woman, the *direct* approach had to be done away with entirely in favor of the *ricocheted* approach. It's all very simple. When one encounters the unattainable beauty, he forgoes all communication with her and instead endears himself to her friend. In this case, it meant rubbing shoulders with Tracy, who really had put on some weight since the last time I saw her, and who was standing alone in the kitchen with a red cup. I walked over to join her.

"Tracy," I started, carefully, "this party is perfect, and I'm really feeling the DJ, too!"

"Thanks! And oh well, you know he's single...?"

"I didn't mean it that way! I'm straight." I was honestly caught off guard by her comment and was thankful no one else had heard her. Still, that she even mentioned it so comfortably meant that someone had started a rumor. I wondered how it had begun. Had someone misinterpreted my social media, my lack of pictures posted for the sole purpose of cultivating a branded life?

"Oh, I'm sorry. You know, no one can ever tell these days." She paused and put her cup down, looking serious for a moment. "Adrian, I'm drunk," she said, and burst out laughing.

I looked around the kitchen and back into the hallway. More than half the party was shitfaced. Cups covered the ground, and couples were kissing in the kitchen. A girl named Destiny was walking around in a fishnet blouse and black jeans, grinding on every lonely-looking man in sight. With each new partner, she spilled more of her drink onto her jeans. Marcelle was surrounded by a small group of people holding twenty-dollar bills. The DJ, sensing the rising tide of intoxication, switched from classic nineties hip-hop to contemporary ratchet. One man removed his shirt, revealing a torso covered in tattoos. People laughed and cheered him on as he screamed out, "Turn up!"

I turned back to Tracy, who was still covering her face.

"It's your birthday. Get bent. You want to dance?"

She offered me her hand, and I pulled her to a spot on the dance floor that was in plain view for Simone.

I've never been a fan of dancing, especially as it pertains to hip-hop music. I thought it was better to just snap to a given song than actually try to exert myself on the dance floor. Tracy apparently loved to dance (at least while she was drunk), and she got right into position with me, pressing her ass against my crotch and going into that delayed rolling motion known as "grinding." The woman does most of the work; the man is supposed to keep up and remain balanced. He maintains the rhythm while she improvises in the fashion of Charlie Parker. Depending on the intensity of the movement, he might even be allowed to place his hands on her backside or around her waist. Eye contact is unimportant, especially since the woman's head is usually down. The whole thing is a vigorous but empty sex ritual for me, but I have seen couples go from timid to vulgar given the right song and setting.

This what not the case for Tracy and I; it was all a ploy to enrage Simone so that she would be more susceptible to my presence. A few times, we made eye contact. But I didn't hold it for long; just long enough for her to know that I was dancing with Tracy but looking for her. We danced through three songs; the last one was Tyga's "Dope." After that, Tracy went right over to Simone to tell her how tired and hot she was.

"Girl, you getting it in out there tonight, I see you!" I heard Simone say. Was she pretending to be proud of Tracy when she seemed secretly jealous?

"Ha ha! Turn up!" she shot back and half-stumbled back into the kitchen for another drink. Another song started. It was Trippie Redd, and the entire party rushed to the dance floor, one throbbing tide of black skin under red lights. It looked obscene. It looked sexy. It felt religious. Everyone went into a spasm. The bass was thick, and the windows were covered with steam. I walked right up to Simone without saying a word and pulled her to dance with me. With the right timing, some women love this.

We were face-to-face but separate, and I could smell the rum on her lips. It was crowded. As people created a beeline behind her to the kitchen, I caught her from falling and pulled her right next to me. She grabbed me and held on tight like she was afraid to let go. She got closer. She was sweating. Her scent was powerful, and we were rocking to the song madly. We should have been barefoot and naked among spears. My hand found a resting place on the small of her back. My other hand held an empty cup. I dropped the cup to the ground and kicked it somewhere. She put a hand around my neck. People were bumping into us, and we were bumping into them. After the song was over, I asked Simone if she remembered saying goodbye to me on the 3 train. She did. I asked her how she knew my name. She said she found out from Marcelle.

"How do you know Marcelle?"

She gave me a confused look and said, "Because that's my man."

Chapter Four

MY ENCOUNTER WITH CONTESSA TAUGHT ME THE FUTILITY OF AN IMPASSIONED IMAGINATION when it came to matters of the heart. Although it is the most delicious feeling to fall freely into worshipping the object of one's affections, this is a trap that leads to instability and heartache. But it is a trap that one chases down regardless. To drown in love is the sweetest death.

It should go without saying that I had to cut off all contact with Marcelle. Whether he knew about my approach to Contessa or not was irrelevant; I had embarrassed myself fantastically. Becoming mesmerized by someone, following someone, only then—just at the moment when she notices you—to be emotionally, psychologically, and spiritually murdered by that same person? I was forced into a long retreat wherein I avoided all parties, chose the emptiest train cars, and fell into an agonizing mood of masturbation. I ate sandwiches every day and went to bed at nine p.m. This attempt to turn the days into a blur was interrupted once when I spotted Contessa and Marcelle from a distance exiting a café on Stuyvesant. I pulled my hat down over my face and changed directions. They couldn't have noticed me, because I turned before they looked my way. Marcelle was grinning piggishly at her hips while he held the door open. After that, I didn't leave my room for five days.

Those five days were spent in a state of suspended animation in front of my phone screen. I didn't even try to use my desktop. The smartphone's slenderness, its lightweight body, its screen's luminescence, were all soothing in an almost maternal sense. I liked how the screen's brightness could be adjusted so that it put just enough strain on the eye at night to carry me away to sleep softly. But then, ten minutes away from a dream, I would hear the jingle of a notification and my eyes would snap open as if soldiers had crashed through my door. With my phone in my hand, I could stay up until maybe three in the morning waiting for updates and tweets and new pictures of girls back in Virginia. Some nights, I would get texts and actually feel happy about it: someone wants to talk to *me*? Someone's thinking about *me*? And I started to fall in love with getting text messages at 2 a.m. I went from leaving my phone on the nightstand to leaving it under the pillow to placing it just beside my head.

During my five-day shut-in, I received another party invitation from Marcelle. Another house party, the event was to be thrown on the upcoming Saturday. But of course I couldn't take the chance of being seen by Contessa, let alone Contessa *and* Marcelle together. *Fuck that!* I thought. In a fit of paranoia, I wondered if the invitation was Marcelle's sly way of getting me to show up somewhere so that he could gloat about me trying to get at his girl. Maybe Contessa hadn't mentioned it, but I couldn't take the chance. And just seeing Contessa would have probably led me into another week of isolation. I ignored the text altogether.

The Saturday of the party, I awoke and went straight to the bathroom mirror. My face was beginning to look hollow. The only food I'd had all week was Top Ramen, and I thought I looked haunted. Embarrassment, or rather the fear of embarrassment, had led to this dehydration of my self. I shared the bathroom with a tenant one floor above mine. His name was Randall. Having lived in the building long before me, he had decorated the bathroom to his liking. There were little Hot Wheels racing cars lined up along the top of the sink's mirror and piles of ancient, scentless potpourri in the corners beside the toilet. The shower curtains were plain white until you looked at their bottoms, which were black with crud. He used a series of bath towels to cover the floor in place of mats, all of which were filthy and uninviting to the bare feet. But worst of all was the small towel he kept at the edge of the sink to catch the toothpaste that fell from his mouth whenever he brushed. This perpetually moist towel was pockmarked with white stains that made me nauseated whenever I had to use the sink.

Early on, thinking that he might have left the towel there by accident, I hung it up on a nearby rack. What sweet bliss it was to see the clean white porcelain beneath. The sink was beautiful, and, after brushing my own teeth, I took extra care to wipe away the drops of water I'd left behind. I even sprinkled a little Ajax on the surface and wiped it again. The porcelain and the faucet shimmered. But Randall would not have any of it. When I made it home again that evening, the moist towel had been placed on the sink again. It featured even larger blotches of toothpaste and emitted the subtle odor of mold. I never touched the towel again. I brushed my teeth with my back facing the mirror until it was time to spit, which I did with my eyes closed. I only knew where the drain was based on the intensity of the moldy smell. I rarely saw Randall, but when I did I got the feeling that he was plotting his revenge against me for touching his towel.

Outside, winter was beginning to strip the trees and infect the skies with its cruel greyness. Had a people ever worshipped winter? Part of me wanted to, but winter itself would not stand for it. Better to move along with haste. I walked to the train and watched the little clouds of my breath evaporate between my steps. I tried to enjoy the creeping numbness in my ears and the rust-colored leaves along my path, but it all spoke of solitude. The trees that still had some of their foliage looked tired and impatient for snow. They stood stiff and ready for the last rainstorm that would finally leave them completely nude. I was hungry, and the train came immediately and full of passengers dressed in black. When I came up from the station, it was night, and I followed a path of streetlights to a grocery store that welcomed me with warmth and stalls full of pumpkins.

The great problem of grocery shopping in Brooklyn came from the tension between seeking out the affordable and the healthy. If I went to a grocery store frequented by the long-time residents of Bed-Stuy, I would have to go strictly vegan, but even this was dangerous. Once, inside a rotten little market on Myrtle, I noticed a small kitten pawing around in the produce section. The cat had wandered in from the back area where the groceries were first received before being brought out to the shelves. The little kitten, perhaps a tabby, was covered in dust as it meandered over the cilantro and carrots. Other shoppers noticed this small outrage but did nothing beyond suck their teeth and move on toward the celery. That no one—including myself—thought to bring this crisis to the attention of the manager was an even larger disaster. In our silence, we accepted the presence of the kitten. Maybe if it were an adult cat we might have been more motivated to say something, but the kitten, with its delicate limbs, looked famished and confused by its apparent orphanage, tumbling around in the vegetables, becoming more enraged at her inability to find any meat. I pushed my cart onward to the frozen section. I bought two small boxes of frozen spinach, one of which I used that same evening. I believe Randall used the other box without my permission.

My own desire for meat kept me away from the cheaper grocery stores because their chicken breasts were sometimes spotted with yellow dye, or else one of the wings in a pack would be badly bruised. Sometimes the beef was brown, and when it wasn't it was somehow *too* red. But if I ventured to a better store, one with fresh pumpkins piled up on stacks of hay, I had to compete with the middle class. Very often what was revolting about these stores that sold Dr. Bronner's soap and organic veal was not only the steep prices but also the frightening herd of shoppers jamming every aisle. Much like the dusty kitten, shoppers pawed at everything helplessly and studied labels. Some aisles were blocked completely by shopping carts designed to hold only two or three items, but I nevertheless endured all of this because being inside that kind of market felt right. To be in the presence of so much pristine abundance, such frenzy over wellness, to be surrounded by the fresh and the farm-raised, inspired the kind of pride one feels when arriving at a party filled with local celebrities and guests whose secrets one knows. Although the market was crowded and being ransacked, in spite of the steep prices and the way some of the customers eyed me worryingly, the smell of olives and fresh fish with lemon mingled in the air around me. I felt I had found a place in the world that looked out for me, that wanted to make sure I was okay, and that confidence, which I rarely felt in front of the computer or at parties or even just walking around the corner to a friend's, was worth everything in my pocket. If I could have given more, I would have. I stepped up to the cashier's register after being directed there by a number on a screen and paid thirty-two dollars for my two pieces of grass-fed meat.

Back outside, night had fallen, and I was thankful to be shrouded in the darkness. The crowds on the sidewalk made me anonymous. I could have walked right by Contessa without even having to look up. If I had known of an easy way to sabotage the train and cut out the lights in the car, I would have done it. I sat at the end of the car with my bag in my lap and closed my eyes. I even did the little trick of putting my headphones on without playing any music. The car was filling up with more and more passengers, and soon overcoats and shoulder bags surrounded me. No one paid attention to me. I was warm.

I felt myself about to slip into a dream when, from the opposite end of the car, there came a loud commotion. The general murmur of conversation was suddenly interrupted by a boy who yelled out, "—and you can suck my fucking dick, you bitch-ass nigga!" The comment caused a stir among the passengers, whose reactions ranged from utter befuddlement at the vulgarity of the remark to growing anticipation of the mandatory response. All eyes turned toward the boy who had made the comment. He was wearing the customary black Supreme jacket and a bright red vintage Adidas hat with the symbol in white. Amid the growing commotion, it was difficult to tell who the comment was aimed at, though a group of girls identified the boy who'd first yelled out as Rich. The girls were calling out to Rich, in between their laughter, to calm down. When the train reached my stop at Nostrand, a flood of school-aged children surrounding Rich left the train, among them another boy who was removing his backpack. It became apparent that he must have been the aforementioned "bitch-ass nigga," for he wasted no time in calling on Rich to fight. With this announcement, everyone on the platform, including some of the elderly, moved to create a circle perhaps twenty feet in diameter around the fighters. Rich and his opponent began the ritual dance that precedes bouts between high school boys; they raised their fists in their unique fashions and began to pace back and forth nervously, tempting each other to throw the first punch. Among the crowd of onlookers, several people produced phones and began recording the match with much enthusiasm. One of the girls inaugurated the bout by yelling out, "Hit that nigga!" and with that, Rich sent out the first strike, though his opponent was in full expectation of it and dodged it in plenty of time. The force of Rich's swing was miscalculated and did not end in proximity to the younger boy's face. Instead it continued on a haphazard trajectory a few feet away from the face of the boy, who responded with a well-placed jab that caught Rich on the right cheek. The crowd let out a collective moan and then cheered. Some of the onlookers even clapped with approval. But the celebration was somewhat premature, as the jab did little to deter Rich, who responded with his own swinging left fist. That punch met its target and sent the younger boy reeling backward. The crowd caught him, kept him erect, and shoved him back toward the center of the makeshift ring. One old man in attendance held up his own fists in an attempt to show the younger boy how to throw a hook, but his example went unnoticed. The short exchange, coupled with the general frenzy on the subway platform, left the two fighters exhausted as they both resettled themselves some distance away from the other.

The onlookers would have none of it. The crowd clamored for the fight to continue. With weariness, Rich took a defensive stance as the younger fighter lowered his head, bobbing left and right, trying to work his way closer to Rich's chin. Rich sent out a wide jab meant more to check his opponent than to cause damage. The younger boy, sensing Rich's reticence, dove headlong into him, and the pair went crashing to the ground, to the great wonderment of the crowd. Rich lost all advantage and fell victim to a full-on pummeling. After about the seventh direct hit to Rich's face, the crowd intervened and removed the younger boy from a body clinging to consciousness. Rich's hat had somehow found its way onto the subway tracks, where it would remain as a testament to the vanquished. Finally, someone in the crowd called out sharply that the police were to be expected, and a great clearing of the platform took place; Rich was dragged out of sight by an army of hands, the younger boy was ushered triumphantly up the stairs and out into the street. The audience dispersed so rapidly that when the police finally arrived, the platform had been overtaken by an entirely new set of passengers, who were truly unaware that a fight had just taken place.

I left the platform wondering if either of the boys had really wanted to fight at all. I was also astonished by the speed with which the whole ordeal took place; the fight was over before the next train had arrived. Outside, hardly anyone on the street gave the indication that they had just seen someone beaten to the ground. In all reality, the fight was a small embarrassment, but also a ritualistic release for the entire neighborhood. Some events, some of these little organic spectacles, made me feel suddenly alive. To feel embarrassed is also a refreshing experience. Embarrassed why? Because when black people erupt with anger in public (and especially in front of white people), the entire race often feels a collective sense of dishonor. The race sighs, except for the young children who have not been completely reined into their blackness and therefore are the most free from its burden. These mischievous kids put fear in the adults because they are not likely to abide by the rules. The rules are the set of sayings, axioms, adages, lived experiences, and so forth that have given black people some sense of how to remain safe around white people. Respectability Politics 101: how not to get arrested or evicted, how to get a table at a nice restaurant. The kids don't know any of this. I don't think they even have the desire to know until that one inevitable day when the demands of blackness are made clear to them. Some of the children have only been subdued through the use of prisons, favored by the systemic legacy of white supremacy.

Perhaps the fighters themselves were already busy with the evening's next episode: finding something to eat or just simply getting home. There was no more need for me to struggle with the image of a tortured face being pummeled on filthy concrete, so I let it pass out of my mind and crossed the street with my groceries.

In fact, I remembered that nothing was going to truly matter for me until I solved the dilemma of Contessa and now (unfortunately) Marcelle. When I made it back to my apartment, I hid my beef as best I could in the freezer, thankful that Randall didn't seem to be home yet. I sat on my bed and tried to sort out how Contessa could have fallen for someone like Marcelle. It was the classic story of the gentleman losing out to the brute. What deceitful strategy had he used to dumbfound her into his arms? At least my approach was sincere and backed by the promise of goodwill and commitment. Marcelle wouldn't dare think of treasuring anyone, let alone a woman. Is that what she wanted? A standard Stanley Kowalski? The thought made me nauseous. Worse than being unable to attain the object of one's desire is finding that the beloved is nothing but a mirage. It couldn't be the case. I wouldn't have been so drawn to her.

Maybe their relationship was nothing serious. Lots of people get involved in relationships just to pass the time, to get over a little snow spell, to have a body to take them to the movies or to a show in the park. It looks good and healthy to be seen with someone romantically. It raises a person's standing in the eyes of observers. When I walk around with a beautiful woman, I know that other women are wondering what I'm so good at. Men either respect or envy me; either way, I become something higher in their eyes. It happens all the time. People get lonely, and they pair up and soon realize their partner is unfit. The faster they run toward each other, the faster they run away.

Unlike me, Marcelle was a master of the "street holler." To most men, his prowess in this field was a thing to be admired. The combination of wit and the ability to withstand rejection are really the only two things a man needs in order to succeed in the sport. In my own case, I disliked the street holler, not because of any fear of rejection but because I could never abide by displaying myself to so many unworthy candidates. Marcelle, however, seemed to echo Proust, believing that women were merely interchangeable instruments of a temporary pleasure. So, upon seeing Contessa for the first time, he only saw a flute—something to put his lips on, something to tap on in order to produce lovely sounds.

I was different.

Chapter Five

IN THE SUMMER, CONTESSA BLOSSOMED. HER SKIN, BATHED IN SUNLIGHT, HAD REACHED ITS most remarkable brown yet, and the general atmosphere of jubilance running amok throughout the city came to be summarized in her smile. Her legs were showing, and her black hair shimmered.

It was just a small miscalculation on her part. She had only intended to come outside briefly and chat with a new friend in front of her apartment, but the friend, Candice, brought up the idea of going to a local park. How could Contessa say no? It was her first summer in New York, and she had never witnessed such a display of open fire hydrants, ice cream trucks, block parties, and music blaring from cars and apartment windows. Looking in any given direction, she saw clouds of carefree children running in and out of the street, haphazardly chasing after one another, throwing water balloons and shouting obscenities their parents pretended not to hear. Or else she saw buff men in baggy jeans and undershirts walking Rottweilers or pit bulls, shouting into cell phones and generally showing off their excitement for the sun to grace the rest of the street. Every time the door of a corner bodega swung open, Dominican music rushed out, along with maybe a cat that managed to skip back inside before the door closed.

"It's not even a long walk. We can stop and get water from the bodega, too," Candice said, surveying the route ahead through her sunglasses. The park was only five blocks away.

"Yeah, okay. Let's go!"

"Shorty!"

"Mami, come talk to me."

"Damn, you bad."

"Damn, you sexy as fuck!"

"Hey, turn around. Really? Bitch!"

"Hey, poetry..."

"There go wifey!"

"You know she stuck up. Don't be stuck up, boo..."

By the time the girls made it to the park, she had endured no less than eight advances. She had smiled at one who called her "poetry," because he was different—in a pathetic way—but the others she ignored.

Not far from where the girls were about to take their seats, there was Marcelle and one of his friends, Daniel, who had been the one who picked Marcelle up from the bus station when he'd first arrived in New York. Daniel was tall and given to wearing young crewneck T-shirts, and was a kind of henchman for Marcelle. His greatest ambition was to one day slay women in the fashion of his boss, but it was highly unlikely that he would ever do so due to a frightening speech impediment he had developed after having his jaw broken at a party six months before.

"Nigga, I saw this bitch the other day with the fattest ass. This bitch had ass like Kim Kardashian, but her waist was like *this* little. For real, nigga. Bitch know she got ass, too. I was trying to fuck on sight; let a nigga beat that shit up," Marcelle said.

"Word, did you try to holler at her?"

"Hell yeah, I came at that bitch with my A-game. Like, this bitch *have* to let me fuck. She was lying to me, though, talking about she only fuck with other bitches. I was like, 'Nigga fuck that, let me fuck you and your friends.' All them bitches can get the dick."

They both laughed conspiratorially, as though they were smarter than the women who'd been smart enough to dismiss their crude offers.

Daniel looked up and saw Contessa and her friends approaching. He tapped Marcelle.

"What about that one right there?"

"Which one? The one on the left?"

"Yeah, the one with all the ass."

"I'm about to crack that bitch right now, just because. Watch."

They laughed again, convinced of the power of their wit, their ability to manipulate. Marcelle waited for the girls to get closer.

"Oh, they in school. You got to be real 'in-your-feelings' with these kinds of females."

As the ladies came within earshot, Marcelle turned back to Daniel and said, "Wow, man, what a beautiful display of flowers."

Contessa blushed. Marcelle saw her do it. How neatly and quickly the affair began after those words. In a moment, Marcelle was working his way up to asking for Contessa's phone number as Daniel expertly struck up a supporting conversation with Candice, intending to keep her from rushing Contessa. He learned that Candice had come to Brooklyn from Denver some eight months before and that she worked at a food co-op. Nothing interesting would come from her Denverness, but a food co-op might be worth something. Daniel logged this information to share with Marcelle later on. Contessa was at her best when she was able to talk about her interests. Her great ambition was to be a photographer in the line of Carrie Mae Weems. She would make Brooklyn her setting and hone in specifically on black women.

"Yeah, you know? Last winter I saw this homeless lady walking in the snow with no shoes. It was heartbreaking, but it would have made a great picture," Marcelle said cautiously.

"Oh no! I mean, I have hundreds of pictures of black women pushing strollers, waiting in lines, sitting in hair salons—but I need to get some pictures of them cooking and kissing, too," Contessa explained.

"That would be awesome!"

"Yeah, so what do you do?

"I'm putting an application together for Harvard. I want to study for my PhD in African history."

This bit of information struck right at the soul of Contessa, who, as she was wont to admit to herself very often, had a "thing for intellectual dudes." Unknowingly, she had slipped that much deeper into the clutches of a self-proclaimed anti-intellect; Marcelle was proud of the fact that he had done away with the reading of books the moment he dropped out of college. He believed books were tools of confusion and that the best men were those who always acted on gut instinct alone. While he was still in school, he'd taken a liking to Thoreau and excerpted passages from Hemingway and Twain, but he hated, above all, the work of the Harlem Renaissance, which he felt was too soft and beggarly, what with its constant appeal to the white gaze and its nauseating self-consciousness. Then again, most books bored him, and he was happy to do away with assigned reading lists in order to dedicate himself wholeheartedly to the sale of MDMA and cocaine and OG Kush.

Contessa had no notion of Marcelle's deep-seated distaste for all things literary as she asked him a few dreamy questions about his interests in African history, revolving around what books he'd read on the topic, if he'd ever been to the Continent, and what he thought of the current situation in the newly formed Eastern African Republic.

The only plane Marcelle had ever been on was the one that took him from California to New York, but to her question about visiting Africa, he said that he had been to Namibia. Windhoek was actually where he wanted to spend some more time researching the topic for his doctorate: the Herero genocide. He knew that Namibia was one of the more obscure nations of Africa. More people knew about Sudan because its genocide was more recent, or Kenya because it too had been in the news recently for a mall shooting, but the early-twentieth-century crimes against the Herero were not big news in America. They had only made a recent splash in Germany after the government decided to acknowledge its culpability for them. Marcelle knew this because he had grown interested in Namibia after watching *Mad Max: Fury Road* and searching for the movie's filming location.

His other replies carried notes of boredom, hinting at hidden interests that Contessa could not help but wonder about beneath all of her questions. As she spoke with him, she felt herself growing warmer. The intensity of her line of questioning was gradually disarmed by Marcelle's cool replies. When the conversation showed signs of exhausting itself completely, Marcelle perked up suddenly and said, "Well, it was real nice to meet you. You're really cool peoples."

"You are, too."

"Me and my boy about to head to the train, though, so let me hit you up a little later on. You got a phone number?"

"Okay. I mean, yes. I do."

A week later, the two met up for an outdoor film screening of *Ghostbusters II* in Herald Square, where they shared a bottle of Gewürztraminer and made jokes about the different sizes of their toes. After the movie, they walked down Sixth Avenue with no particular destination in mind, stopping occasionally to take pictures or to gaze into shop windows. Contessa was especially fond of the pet store with its Pomeranians and Yorkies vying for attention. She took a picture of Marcelle tapping on the glass and making faces at the excited puppies. They ended up eating slices of pizza together; Marcelle had a plain slice, while Contessa ordered a slice with roasted red peppers and artichoke.

"Mine is too hot," Marcelle said, jerking the fuming pizza away from his mouth.

"Have a bite of mine."

The very next night, Marcelle insisted that going into the city would be a hassle, so they agreed to stay at her place and watch a movie. During the movie, perhaps ten minutes in, Marcelle placed his hand inside Contessa's left thigh so that the side of his palm was pressed firmly against her pussy. He let his hand stay there after Contessa shifted cautiously to make the contact more comfortable. They kissed briefly but passionately and forgot about the movie altogether.

From here, they became almost inseparable. They enjoyed every moment they spent together, and, when they parted, they sent text messages back and forth for hours at a time. The days went by. The seasons changed. They made love, argued passionately, and then made better love. Marcelle inspired a new set of dreams and fantasies in her. She cooked and danced delicately around his agitations, and in return he stayed faithful, truly honoring her when he was alone or with friends and other women made passes at him. Her love for Marcelle grew like some great vine sprawling with so much urgency over the walls of her heart. It was love, true love, though she believed it, while he only stated it. Contessa's friends were completely convinced of the meaningfulness of their union. Secretly, Marcelle would wonder how he had allowed himself to get so close to Contessa, why he hadn't managed to pull away after the first time they had sex. She was starting to take things too seriously, he thought. Still, her body was incredible, and she looked good.

One evening when they were together, Marcelle felt especially attracted to Contessa and seized her in his arms right in the middle of her talking. He kissed her and started removing her clothes. She consented, smiling at his cunning. She'd convinced herself that he was even more attractive when he was aggressive, like it was tangible proof of his desire.

She gave herself over completely. She stopped trying to steer and control anything and leapt off the edge of a great canyon onto a bed of roses a mile thick. Seven weeks later, she discovered that she was pregnant.

Marcelle was seated at a bar with Daniel when the text message arrived.

> We need to talk. ASAP.
> Where r u?

Marcelle paid for his drink and excused himself from the bar. Daniel laughed over his beer, saying, "Oh, you know you must be in trouble now!" Marcelle smiled, but he was frowning once he stepped outside. "This is why I hate bitches," he mumbled to himself as he crossed the street. He had no idea that Contessa was about to tell him about her pregnancy. He figured the text message was really just a ploy to get him to stop having fun away from her. An encroachment on his "me" time, that special zone that men require for rejuvenation, self-analysis, and masturbation. When he knocked on her front door, she was in a robe and holding a pregnancy test. She immediately blurted out, "I'm pregnant."

His former chivalry gave way to a quiet panic. He was a great monument crashing down to the earth. His face was raw and motionless, but his eyes revealed all the boyish fear that was bursting forth inside him.

"Why are you just looking at me like you don't have anything to say?"

"I mean. I don't know what to say."

"You weren't this quiet when you were helping to make it."

"Well..."

"Well, what?"

"What do you want to do?"

"Well, of course I'm not going to have it."

"Okay."

At that announcement, Marcelle felt a strange mixture of relief and abandonment. One part of him was comforted by the fact that his sexual escapades would not have to come to a halt in the name of fatherhood. The other part, however, felt as though his very manliness had been neutralized. To think that

Contessa had made such a critical decision so quickly and without really needing to hear his input made his penis feel worthless and his charm seem childish. He thought back to all of the women he could remember sleeping with and pained himself with wondering whether or not each of them had this same capacity to render him irrelevant. For a very brief moment, he thought about becoming celibate and spending a year or two trying to understand the meaning of sex. But, very quickly, he remembered that Contessa was *not* going to have the baby, and he suppressed his emotions and became happy again. He began to shed the old charming skin and emerged as an even more cunning seducer right there in front of Contessa. He hugged her and told her that he loved her. She began to cry in his arms. He kissed her. The robe was removed, and they made love again.

After having twice exhausted himself with Contessa, Marcelle rolled over in bed and quickly fell asleep. As he snored, Contessa lay there turning over the prospect of an abortion. Would she really go through with it? Should she call home and tell her parents—at least her mother—what was happening? No! It would only bring unnecessary concern, and after all she had come to New York to be a *real* adult, not an adult-in-training the way she had been during college, what with the deposits to her account sent from home and her father coming to the campus every year to help her move into a new dorm. She'd found her New York room, a job, and saved up for the deposit all on her own and without any input from her family. She reminded herself that plenty of women must have the operation every day and that the alternative was unacceptable. She couldn't raise a child with Marcelle. She knew that he was going to be trouble sooner or later if he hadn't already started. He never took any pains to hide that fact that he sold drugs. Plenty of evenings, he poured out the contents of his stash on her desk. Sometimes she wondered if criminals or police would ever follow him into her room one day. She was only half joking when she had those thoughts, but with a child in the picture the thought became an omen. Marcelle was an irresistible kind of trouble, a kind of sweet and amorphous syrup, always moving to envelop her slowly. And what could the victim do but swim helplessly? Still, being caught up in someone for a moment of pleasure was not the same as being attached at the expense of a new life. She was tempted to pull out her phone and google "abortion procedure" followed by "does an abortion hurt," but she was afraid to see the results.

Then her thoughts moved to the possibility of raising a child without Marcelle. Who was she to end the baby's chance to live? She was certain that plenty of children were born to broken families who went on to grow up and become major successes, motivated by their disadvantage. A boy going to the NBA would be acceptable, if not a tad cliché, but even better would be a child making it to Harvard Law School. Or it would be a girl, who would grow up both resenting and longing for her absent father; she would excel in all school subjects, leave the state for college and eventually enroll in Harvard. Everything following that would be a cascade of success: she would marry someone—perhaps a white man—who was rich and interested in her mother's photography. But the thought of not being discovered until her daughter found a suitable husband made her shiver, and she focused instead on being a poor, single black mother with a known seducer as the baby's father. A life filled with EBT lines and loud neighbors would have to be hers until the child was out of high school.

Moving back and forth between the two imagined fates was becoming too heavy. Contessa sat up expressionless and looked down on Marcelle, who was still snoring, and briefly considered stabbing him in the face. When he woke up an hour later, she was gone.

Far from feeling any degree of panic, Marcelle was relieved by her absence and quickly set about going through his contacts to see if there were any women in his phone who would be available to cook for him. Ashley was currently out of town, Ariel had recently started a new relationship, Aze was a complete disaster in the kitchen (she nearly burned down her parents' house on four separate occasions), Bianca was a good cook, but he wanted black people food, so he settled on Brianna, who was, among other things, a master of flour and hot grease. He called her.

"Hello?"

"What you doing, boo?"

"Hi, Marcelle."

"You mad?"

"I just haven't heard from you in a while. What's wrong?"

"Nothing is wrong. I'm trying to see you right now."

"Oh, you must be hungry?"

"Not just for food."

"You think you're so slick. I'm at work," Brianna said after giggling.

"Let me come see you tonight then."

"Wow. I don't get off until ten. I'm gonna be tired. Plus, I have a boyfriend now."

"I told you before, I don't like labels."

"You know what I mean!"

"Well, I want to hang out with you for a little bit, I'm talking to someone now, too."

"Who?"

"We're not about to get into all of that."

"Yeah, right. I'm going to call you when I get off," she said excitedly.

"Okay."

"And please answer the phone."

"Okay."

There was about an hour left before Marcelle would have to leave to meet up with Brianna. He sat back down on the bed wondering what he should do to occupy the time. His eyes traveled around the room, stopping briefly on each of the little articles and personal effects that made up Contessa's life. On a wall, near the only window in the room, there was a series of photographs. He remembered looking at them for a moment the first time he'd come to visit her, but he'd taken no real interest in them until now. He stepped over and eyed them carefully. Each picture depicted a topless black woman seated alone in a chair holding an article of food. In the first picture, a rather tall woman sat holding a plum with both hands. Her hair was braided into two thick and bushy pigtails. She stared blankly into the camera, her face filled with freckles.

"That bitch look like a mulatto," he said to himself, pondering over the splash of dots on her face. None of the portrait subjects looked over twenty-one. In the fourth picture, he recognized Candice's face. She was holding a bowl of rice, but her breasts were not nearly as tempting as all the others. She had a small mole just above her belly button.

"Is my bitch a lesbian?" he wondered. "What if she came to my spot and saw a bunch of pictures of niggas' dicks all over the wall?"

The women looked unhappy. Each held her dish with a soft expression of submission tinged with reluctance at being so fully exposed. Marcelle was annoyed; he felt that each picture would have been better if only the women were fully undressed and smiling.

No longer interested in the picture series, he circled the room slowly, weighing whether or not to get a better idea of Contessa's honesty by rummaging through the imposing chest of drawers on the other side of the room. He paused. Had he come across something unsavory or too revealing, he might have lost his cool demeanor. He was dealing with a volatile situation. Contessa was a pregnant woman who had just decided to have an abortion without any of his input. She might decide to go back on her decision at the slightest infraction. If he remained calm and neutral, she would be more motivated to follow through with her first mind.

Besides, he also knew he was a monster, and she sensed it. No woman in her right mind would spend much time contemplating Marcelle as a potential father. She knew he was a cheater, a liar, a dog, and a scumbag who had no intention whatsoever of pursuing a Ph.D. from Harvard. Part of her ignored the deception, but people can only ride a train of lies so far before they have to jump off and crash to the ground below. An abortion, he thought, was a clean slate.

Contessa was brilliant, a true rogue of genius, he thought, to make such a life-affirming choice. He began to long for her curly hair, which gave off the aroma of lavender when they made love with the covers pulled over their heads at night. Atop her chest of drawers sat a picture of her in her graduation cap and gown from Vassar. If only she were in the room, wearing the long black gown, biting her bottom lip in invitation. Sex with Contessa was a courageous act, one had to be both amenable and intense; she laughed when Marcelle pulled her hair. It was bewildering at first, but he grew to love her enticing antics. She could be ferocious, even tyrannical with her demands for gratification, but if they were met, she became docile and acquiescing in her own right, bent on making herself a tool of his pleasure. He concluded that the orgasms with Contessa were indispensable and that, as such, he must do everything in his power to keep her in his good graces even after the abortion.

Finally fed up with the apartment, he grabbed his hat and left. At the end of the block, in front of the corner store, there was a muddled cloud of alcoholics sharing cigarettes and exchanging neighborhood gossip about car thefts and recent arrests. They were also sizing him up to see if he would spare any change. Marcelle never gave money to beggars. His mantra was: *Every grown, healthy nigga should work for his money. I only give money to women.* One out of the bunch stepped forward with yellow eyes and dried snot caked around his nostrils and put out his palm.

"Help me out, boss, you know I ain't had a beer all day."

"Can't do it, bro," Marcelle said curtly, without breaking eye contact with the door handle.

"Bullshitting-ass little nigga," the old drunk mumbled. A layer of tobacco-choked mucus crowded his throat.

There was no relief in the store. About nine other men of various ages were inside, hanging out and shooting the shit with one another and taking turns trying to convince the Dominican shopkeeper, Yoskar, to hand over a free beer or cigarettes on credit.

"Come on, motherfucker, give me a Thunderbird or just one of these little Budweiser cans," one of them called out, wobbling up to the counter.

"No, you already drunk enough, why you need more for?"

"Aw, you full of shit, Yos, you full of shit. Can't give a nigga a break, hot as is it outside? Won't even cut the air condition on high for me, you see we in here sweating. I come in here for twenty years buying shit— paper towel, cat food, all that bullshit—and you won't let him have one little drink till I pay you back. Shit! Let me get some coffee then."

"Okay, get you one cup, Papi."

"Nigga, I don't want no hot-ass coffee, it's a hundred and fifty-two degrees in here. I want a beer, goddammit!"

Everyone laughed except Marcelle, who wanted his own beer and condoms. After several more minutes of appeals, the drunk was finally given one can of Budweiser, at which point he promptly left the store. Marcelle paid for his own items and went back outside.

He walked down Milton Street toward Fulton where Brianna lived. To his right, there was a small park with a set of basketball courts, games being played on each one. Marcelle stopped for a moment to watch. He admired the players and considered joining in but dismissed the thought. He didn't know anyone on the court. After all, he wasn't from the neighborhood. It really shouldn't have mattered; he was young and had enough skill to contribute to any team. But no one had invited him. "You don't walk up to groups like that when you're all alone," he thought. Besides, where would he put his bag to ensure that no one stole what was inside?

Night rolled over the tops of the brownstones, and as the streets darkened they grew more active. Marcelle felt good just walking along amid the noise and voices bouncing from different directions, families calling out to one another in the moist heat. He thought about Contessa briefly but managed to push those thoughts out of his mind, instead choosing to focus on the arguments and ecstasies of the people in the streets. One family had pulled a grill out into the front of their home, and smoke billowed up past the blacked-out windows above. Two police officers, walking their beat, stopped at the house and spoke to the man at the grill. Unable to hear the conversation, Marcelle watched as the cook spoke with upraised hands and smiled at the officers.

"Probably snitching," he said to himself as he hurried along toward Fulton, not wanting to draw any attention to his backpack. He pulled out his phone and saw that he'd missed a call from Brianna. He was only a few blocks away from her apartment.

Brianna had neglected to tell Marcelle that she would be having other guests over that night as well. She had invited friends—all of whom she had met recently in New York—over for drinks, not because she wanted to play host to new people, but because she wanted to create a buffer between herself and Marcelle. By hosting a small party, she would be able to keep herself from being persuaded to sleep with him, as her story about "talking to someone" had been a tactic to try and get Marcelle to take his mind off of her bedroom. It wasn't a matter of losing her desire for Marcelle that made her put up this defense; she only wanted to check his hubris. Before Marcelle met Contessa, back when he was seeing Brianna on a weekly basis, he had crossed the line during one of their outings. He made a scene in the lobby of a movie theater, complaining that Brianna had not been affectionate enough during the film, that the only two things her mouth was good for were screaming out his name and stuffing itself with popcorn. The outburst attracted the attention of a security guard, who promptly escorted the drunken Marcelle outside, leaving Brianna with a near-empty bag of popcorn, embarrassed and standing alone. She was far from heavyset; it was the seriousness with which she ate that bothered Marcelle. He couldn't help but think she consumed her food with the urgency of a dog, dropping bits and crumbs into her lap and allowing the sound of her breathing to become audible. Marcelle figured that it must have been a habit developed during her childhood, because she was raised with four brothers in poverty. It was all so disappointing and heartbreaking for Marcelle, who had come to distinguish her as his best catch but who also found her to be his greatest embarrassment.

He was stunned when Brianna opened the door and he saw the small group of people sitting around in the living room. Everyone turned to look at him as he stepped in with the black plastic bag with beer and condoms inside.

At least there's two new girls in here, he thought as he smiled and waved cheaply at everyone. After removing his shoes, he walked the bag straight into the kitchen without being told. Brianna was annoyed by his show of familiarity, but he was, after all, the person whom she knew best out of the bunch. She felt that her strategy for keeping him at bay was already beginning to fail.

When he came back to the living room, Brianna introduced him. "Everyone, this is my friend Marcelle, we went to college together. Marcelle, that's Emmanuel, Kelvin, and 'Demetrius,' right? Right! And Nandi and Tiffany," she said as introduced the group.

"Cool. It's nice to meet everyone. So what's been going on?" asked Marcelle as he took a seat in the chair Brianna had been sitting in.

"We were all in here talking about applying to school." Emmanuel spoke up as he poured himself a drink. "I want to go back for my master's in comparative lit, but I'm not sure where to apply. Kind of worried about the loan thing, too."

"I told him he should just go straight into the Ph.D. program, at least they have funding," Demetrius added. He appeared to be the most successful out of everyone; he was wearing a tie. Marcelle eyed him suspiciously.

Brianna asked if anyone wanted another drink. The two women held out their cups, and Marcelle asked specifically for whiskey, which is what he saw at the bottom of Demetrius's cup. When she came back with the drinks, Marcelle drank his in one gulp and immediately asked for another, this time with more liquor. He claimed he needed to catch up with the group, and this made everyone laugh. Brianna was losing more ground.

"The thing is, if you go to a top school," Demetrius began again, "a really quality school like Harvard, you won't have to worry about paying anything. Those schools have reputations. They can't afford to be blemished with word of their students being so impoverished by student loan payments that they can't lead comfortable lives. The problem is that people sell themselves short in the application process and end up somewhere like a cash-strapped HBCU or some money-hungry academic assembly line like NYU when those schools do everything in their power to ruin their students with loans."

"I can see that," Emmanuel added meekly.

"I don't know, though," Tiffany broke in. "NYU is a pretty good school. Plus, a lot of these Ivy League schools only accept, like, ten students per program, and there's, like, thousands of people applying every year so you kind of have to apply to a bunch of schools."

"Right, and just because the school is Ivy League doesn't mean it has the best program in a particular field," said Nandi, slightly annoyed by Demetrius. Marcelle began watching her reactions more closely.

Kelvin, who had just made his way back from the kitchen with one of the beers bought by Marcelle, jumped into the fray. "School, school, school. There's no jobs, and it costs too much money. Why bother?" Marcelle gave him an admiring nod.

"Honestly, that's what people say who majored in film," Demetrius decided. He and Kelvin had been roommates in college.

"Whatever," said Kelvin, smiling into his bottle as he took a seat on one of the couches. Over the years, he had become accustomed to bowing out gracefully during debates with his former roommate.

"Seriously, though, how can people complain about not being able to find a job when you have a degree in photography?" Demetrius's annoyance was plain.

Marcelle thought back to the pictures in Contessa's bedroom. He was beginning to feel the whiskey and asked Brianna for another drink. She made it for him without hesitating.

"Okay, so what do you guys think about this one?" Brianna suddenly exclaimed. "This shit happened to my friend." Some of the wine fell out of her glass and onto the wooden floor. She went for a paper towel as she continued her story. "My friend Nicole got into a Ph.D. program at Fullerton in comparative lit, fully funded for four years. She spent six years in the program, totally confused about why she was there, then dropped because she couldn't take it anymore. She said she felt dumb every day that she was in the program."

"She finally did something smart," Marcelle said, placing his glass down on the table in front of him. There was still some whiskey inside of it.

"Is Nicole black?" asked Demetrius.

"Yeah."

"Most black people just aren't cut out for PhD programs, unless it's in Black Studies or something."

"Damn, that's harsh," Kelvin said.

Marcelle was surprised that Demetrius had finally said something he agreed with. "It's true," he said. "I dropped out of school during my sophomore year of college because I knew it wasn't worth it."

"So what do you do now?" Nandi asked, suddenly taking an interest in him.

"I make money," he said quickly before turning to Demetrius. "And also, I don't think *being black* has anything to do with not being able to finish the program. I think most people aren't really ready for that kind of commitment. The real issue is everyone thinking *school* is the only way to succeed in life."

"So you just dropped out with no plans to ever try to go back?" Demetrius put in, rudely.

"I'm done with school forever," Marcelle answered dismissively. Then, growing more resolute, he continued, "I left all that behind a while ago because I figured out it just wasn't worth it. They not interested in educating me, they interested in breaking my pockets. They didn't teach me nothing in school except how easy it was to cheat on a test. All the classes were bullshit." He took another sip from his cup.

"Well, not *all* of the classes? Some of them have to be worth something," Kelvin poured beer into his own cup.

"The classes don't add up to anything. They let you go in there and take Intro to African American Studies, then you take Intro to European History, then you take Chinese Lit I, then you take Golfing, but none of it is really talking about what you're learning in your other classes, like, how to make it all come together and actually mean something other than collecting trivia facts for *Jeopardy*. So college is just like flipping through a bunch of channels on cable; you get a lot of variety, some of it's interesting, but it never adds up to anything. Same way people get bored with TV, that's how I got bored with college."

"But that's what school *should* be!" Kelvin replied. "You should be able to pick and choose what you want to learn. I mean, I *am* paying for it, I should have a say in what I'm taught."

"No, your parents are probably paying for your education, or the federal government is. And how the hell is the average dumbass eighteen-year-old supposed to really know what they need to be taking to get a quality education? Be wasting time taking classes like Intro to Sonic the Hedgehog and don't know which amendment freed the damn slaves."

"The Thirteenth Amendment."

Jeopardy-ass nigga, Marcelle thought.

"That's just extreme," Emmanuel grumbled disdainfully.

"What is?"

"That people are taking Sonic the Hedgehog."

"You can label it whatever you want, but you can't deny the fact that there are a bunch of fluff courses in school."

"I don't know what gives you so much authority to speak on the state of academia when you dropped out after freshman year, though," Demetrius suddenly fired back. "I think you're kind of bitter."

"Bitter?"

"Yeah, I think you might just regret leaving school. I think you miss the classroom."

"Well, see? Here you have the perfect example of the product of a *full* higher education. He can't see that as a result of my dropping out of school, I was able to dodge all that student loan debt, think for myself, and stack chips. Leaving school was probably the best decision I ever made. After all, it wasn't like I wanted to be a damn doctor. And, unlike you, I'm not taking on six-figure debt to get a degree."

"Oh! He went there," Demetrius called out, jerking his cup from his lips.

"I did. And I agree, I think African American studies is probably the most irrelevant degree you can get. People think they gone be W. E. B. Du Bois and ain't even read *Souls*. I think it's just a trendy degree that makes it easy for people to go to school. Nobody respects those degrees unless you're at Harvard or something. When you see a talking head on TV and it says 'Dr. Jamel Peterson, Ph.D., African American Studies, Gunther University,' you immediately have to roll your eyes because you know he's about to start preaching that same old bullshit about 'the Struggle' and 'We Shall Overcome,' old Al-Sharpton-with-a-highlighter-ass nigga."

"Yeah, he's drunk," said Demetrius, wearily.

"No, he isn't, let him have another drink. He's just salty," Kelvin sneered.

The air in the room turned toxic. Marcelle tried not to lose his composure.

"Yeah, man, he's butt-hurt right now because he didn't finish school," Demetrius went on, looking to end the discussion with a final blow. "He's trying to preach to the race, but he probably dropped out of school to sell drugs to the race. Imagine that."

Everyone, including the women, groaned, and Marcelle frowned.

"Wait a minute. For the record, I got kicked out of school for selling weed to people *in college*. It's funny how you niggas want to condemn me for being the dope man when you all probably buy trees every week. And since we're talking about it, I never liked being in school to begin with. You all have degrees and loans, but you have no *chips*. I don't have to lie to people to make it seem like my degree is worth its price. Please, you niggas will always be trapped in debt. You'll always be slaves."

The group erupted into equal parts laughter and mumbling disgust. Marcelle had turned the tide.

"That debt issue is something serious," said Tiffany, shifting in her seat on the couch.

"True," Brianna added.

"This is what I'm talking about," Marcelle said, relieved that he'd made an ally, but wavering from the alcohol. "Everywhere you go, you hear somebody talking about these loans. I think it's a conspiracy to keep everybody in line, to keep everybody begging for a nine-to-five. This is why everybody complains about the music, the books, the movies—it's because nobody is taking the time to be creative and think through things. Everybody just wants a good-paying job to pay back that debt. Nobody's willing to take a risk anymore. Well, except for people like that dude who started Facebook, real niggas like that? He was a risk-taker and ended up creating a company that everybody uses to feel good about their boring lives. The risk-takers are the ones innovating and running the world and creating algorithms, while everybody else is whining and cosigning on the Internet."

"Yeah, but everyone can't be Mark Zuckerberg," Emmanuel said. "You can't expect everyone to just drop out of school and start making websites. I think the real problem is people like you who want immediate success and don't understand the time that really needs to go into earning anything worthwhile and stable. I mean, sure, you're making money and you don't have any debt now, but how long do you think your little operation can last? What happens when you get caught up and have to blow your savings on bail money? It happens all the time."

"Yeah, what about your retirement? What about that 401(k)?" Kelvin blurted out, happy that Emmanuel had cut Marcelle's rant short. It was beginning to make him feel uncomfortable.

Before Marcelle could reply, Brianna said, "I just don't think it's so black-and-white? Some people actually *have* to go to college, doctors and lawyers and stuff, right? I think the main issue with today is not that everyone is going to school instead of 'innovating,' like Marcelle said, it's that the schools are charging way too much, especially in this economy that doesn't have enough jobs available."

"Yes, you better be the sensible one, Bri," Nandi called out triumphantly as she reached for her glass of wine.

"There's really only one person here who isn't being sensible," muttered Demetrius.

Marcelle stood up, with some effort, and asked squarely, "Nigga, do you got a problem?"

"Oh, no," said Brianna suddenly, "not in my apartment, I just got the lease. No. Sorry, Marcelle, you have to go. I can't have all of that in here."

"Get this dude out of here before he hurts himself. Damn drunk," said Demetrius.

"Oh, I get it, Bri. This who you talking to now? That's why he feel so special? Whatever. I'll leave. I ain't mad. I already finished that. Nothing really left in the bottom of that glass," Marcelle said drunkenly.

"Marcelle, please, you have to go!"

He took one more sip from his glass and sat it down ceremoniously. His phone was vibrating. Behind him, he could hear everyone whispering dismissals of him. As he made it out the front door, he saw that Contessa had sent him a text message. He had missed seven of her calls.

After waiting for more than an hour, Contessa finally received a reply from Marcelle. In her last message she had asked him where he was, how could he leave her alone in her condition, and finally she told him that she couldn't be alone. Marcelle's reply was simple: almost there.

She was not certain that seeing Marcelle would actually help her feel any better. It felt customary, she thought, to have him around and she tried sorting out the meaning of her decision. Earlier, after she had first left Marcelle sleeping in her room, she made the necessary arrangements to end the pregnancy. She was set on a date, she'd withdrawn enough cash from her checking account to put aside for the appointment, and she told one friend (Candice) everything that was going to happen. It was calming when Candice admitted having gone through the same ordeal only a few months earlier: the whole thing was very simple and it would all be over so quickly.

"But do you ever think about the baby?"

"Yes, but not as much as I used to," Candice had confessed.

"So how you doing now?" Marcelle asked, taking a seat on Contessa's bed.

"I don't want to ever have to do this again."

"Do what?"

"You know what."

"You really going to do that?"

"I already told you that I was."

"Yeah, but are you sure?"

"Yes."

They sat together on the bed quietly for a moment. Marcelle put his arm around Contessa, and she leaned against his shoulder. They were quiet for a while longer before Contessa started again.

"It really just goes to show how careless everyone is. Everybody wants to have sex. Everybody wants to feel good. I think it used to be that you had to have a little more invested, even when it was just for a good time. Now you do whatever you want without worrying about what might happen. Right? I'll have kids when I'm ready. It's my body—there's a little bit of you involved, but it's mainly me. I even thought about naming him after you."

"How do you know it's a boy?"

"I just know. But I can't do that. It's just not right. I have things I need to do. I wish it was you that had to have it done, but it's not."

"Do you still want to be with me after?"

"No. I want us to go to my friend's birthday party together next week, and after that, you live your life and I'll live mine."

"Then it was settled," Marcelle thought. Contessa had figured everything out without him again. He was secondary. Naturally, it made her more attractive to him. It was a strange, engrossing feeling to be conquered that way; she had outmaneuvered him. She looked calm sitting there explaining how they would never be together or make love again.

Unlike my rival and all the boys she loved before, I could have loved Contessa. I could have been with her and laughed about things and never let her feel lonely. I didn't care what happened in her past. I fell in love with Contessa Thursday morning on the 3 train into the city. Her past was a great wide nothing to me. I had a past, too, filled with agitating encounters and uncomfortable mix-ups with ugly women. (Very few women are actually "ugly." It's just the ones that agitate me, and very few women have ever made me feel that way.) But none of them ever stirred up my insides the way Contessa did. People like Marcelle who go about dismantling refined machinery, stomping through painstakingly arranged gardens, and doing their very best to vandalize the last beautiful things we humans have, these people should be punished and humiliated in public squares; medieval justice for careless womanizers and a bed of flowers for their victims.

Chapter Six

I WOKE UP TO THE SOUND OF A WOODEN TABLE SNAPPING AND CRUNCHING IN THE BACK OF A garbage truck. It's always during the most pacifying dreams that the waking world puts together an orchestra of grating noises to rouse you from your peace. Nothing was worse than the scraping sound of my doorbell, which is why I cut the wire to it. I rarely turned the ringer up on my phone. I kept my windows shut in the summer to try and drown out the noise of car stereos and home entertainment systems, but the bass still rattled my walls. I thought a perfect day for me would include sitting silently with Contessa by my side and maybe a little rain, or, even better, heavy snow so that I wouldn't have to put up with the ruckus of snarling buses and wailing ambulance sirens.

The first thing that I remembered after the sweet image of Contessa had vanished momentarily from my mind was that I was still very poor. I reached for my wallet in the back pocket of a pair of jeans I had hanging on the closet door. It was empty.

At that time, I had a job. I worked as a counselor for drug-abusing high school students. Most of the kids were dropouts trying to finish their GED requirements and remain clean, but I don't think any of them quit using drugs entirely. It was my job to oversee the progress of a small group of students. I visited their homes during the week to help them with their studies and talk to them about any problems they were having. After these meetings, I would add comments about each student to his or her individual file, which then had to be turned in to my boss, Rosa, every two weeks. Rosa's office was on Wall Street, and going to visit her always made me feel very important, even if all the big finance companies had fled lower Manhattan after 9/11, leaving vacancies to be filled by mismanaged nonprofits like the one I worked for. Signing in at the lobby's front desk, taking the elevator to the seventeenth floor, looking at all the workers going back and forth between offices and bathrooms, it gave me the sense that I belonged to something larger and more important than the dreary little world of my room with its Internet and empty, unwashed bowls. It was an easy job, too. Aside from the visits to Rosa, I had complete freedom to arrange my schedule however I liked, so long as I recorded two visits per week with each student. A visit was supposed to last two hours, but I was usually able to leave in fifteen minutes because people don't like house calls from social worker types to begin with. Some of the families were friendlier, but most were happy to see me close my binder and walk out the door. With shortened sessions, I could take on more students, and that meant more money. On average, I made about three thousand dollars a month. If I felt really sinister, I could take home five.

I was broke because I hadn't been to visit any of my students since first becoming obsessed with Contessa. I'd spent the last couple of weeks submerged in the depression of defeat; I started feeling ugly and out of shape, and very few events interested me, but those feelings eventually passed. Reinvigorated, I pledged to get some more money, find Contessa, and show her that she had made a mistake in being with anyone but me.

The rent for my room was due soon, so I had to hurry. Any day, old, evil, plodding Randall was going to come knocking on my door with his ashy fist, asking dryly, "You got the rent?" I was motivated by this and grabbed the necessary folder and paperwork describing the case of Aaron Greene, a marijuana-abusing dropout who was now twenty years old and unable to read much of anything. His forms stated that he had been a masterful dodger of school, having somehow evaded truancy and absence notices for three years. He was only discovered after Mr. Chapman, a teacher who was taking his science class on a field trip to the Natural History Museum, was teased by some of his students for not recognizing "Aaron Greene," whose name had been called every day of the semester without a response. They had just seen Aaron walking on the platform of the C train at Euclid with his mother and younger sister. Embarrassed and uncertain, Mr. Chapman took it upon himself to ask the mother if everything was all right, seeing as how Aaron hadn't been to class in several weeks. Ms. Greene was baffled. Finally captured in this manner, Aaron confessed everything to his mother right there on the platform and reenrolled in school. Later, when it was discovered by his classmates that he was the oldest freshman in the school's 114-year history, he was forced to drop out once more on account of all the jokes being made about his "senior citizen" status. He endured those taunts for two daunting and friendless years, all the while developing an insatiable appetite for weed and cheap cognac. After being called to the principal's office under suspicion of selling weed on campus, he was expelled and recommended for the BRIGHT Program to get his life together.

To get to Aaron's place, I had to take the bus on a solemn journey to the very back of the city, which is East New York. I say that this bus ride was solemn because everybody seemed grimmer once we crossed New Lots Avenue into that neighborhood of barbed-wire fences and burned couches waiting at the curb.

I gathered just enough change from my drawer to cover the bus fare there and back and went out the door quietly so as not to alert the brooding Randall, who I was certain was upstairs with his ear pressed to the door or with his head hovering out over the steps, waiting to catch me as I left. I made it out undetected. Outside, December was approaching, though November was doing its best to keep the inevitable snow at bay. The sky was silver and sunless, but there was still some light. The uninterrupted gray of the clouds looked hard like stone, and I imagined the sky itself cracking and revealing some unfathomable scene behind it, like God in her dressing room. My old friends, the brownstones, stood proudly, ever ready like sentinels on the night watch, all lined up together at the shoulders with their longing, darkened windows forever staring across the streets at each other. Half a block ahead, I saw my bus cross the intersection, so I ran to join the line of passengers queuing up to board. As it turned out, I was ten cents short on the fare, but the bus driver was impatient and unconcerned, agitated by the traffic. He crammed in passengers who were unwilling to make room for the newly boarded. Without even looking at me, he waved his hand as if batting at a gnat and said, "Hurry up."

Everyone on the bus eyed me suspiciously as if my presence meant that they would have to share their already low supply of food. At each stop, two people would get off and ten more would get on. The traffic jam we found ourselves in felt unjustified; there were no accidents, no broken stoplights, just people fighting like rats over a few inches of space in a given lane. In the midst of this congested nightmare, one of the passengers, completely invisible to me, began preaching a fiery sermon on Daniel in the lion's den. The preacher was furious, and his quotation of scripture carried such a dazzling note of sincerity and charisma that some of the passengers couldn't help themselves and yelled "Amen." The preacher's terrifying assault on the sinner came next and was followed by ominous warnings about the return of Christ. A large portion of the congregation soon lost interest, and one enraged passenger yelled out, "Shut the fuck up, please!"

Tension spread throughout the bus; some of the riders sided with the preacher, while the others grew more unsettled. It had gotten so crowded and tightly packed that I was no longer holding onto the rail above my head. I could do nothing but stand up straight and listen to the preaching.

Although I was hedged in from every side, it wasn't claustrophobia that was responsible for my agitation. It wasn't the creeping odor that began to fill the bus or even the general want of personal space. What really bothered me was being unable to get my phone out of my pocket so that I could look at Contessa's profile to see if she'd added any new pictures. If Contessa had been standing there next to me, she would have liked to hear that sermon, and perhaps we would have glanced over at each other and smiled about it, knowing we had just silently established a little inside joke together, something we could bring up later that night or over the phone and laugh about. Although shrewd and cunning, Marcelle did not have the higher type of personality necessary to share brief and delicate moments with people around him. Boorish people like Marcelle were incapable of camaraderie; the unrefined nature of their upbringing and its constant state of paranoia and hunger forced people like Marcelle to rely on banditry and cheap flattery so as to keep everyone around them reeling and off balance, putting him in a position of power, no matter how small or fleeting.

I missed my stop. I was now in an unfamiliar part of Brooklyn because the bus had made a detour around some construction. Everything outside looked miserable, impoverished, vandalized, and shuttered. The sun was setting. I pressed the tape above the rail to get off at the next stop. I was the only person getting off there, and people grunted at me as I squeezed by them to get to the door. Standing on the sidewalk again, I sort of missed the preacher's voice. It was calming, even though his frightening message wasn't. I went for my phone and used the map to find out just how far from Aaron's I was—about six blocks. The important thing was to not look stupid and lost. There were some people hanging around, wobbling in front of a fried chicken spot, pulling on the last bits of cigarettes. Homeless people, winos, hookers, and even dopeheads are generally not a big problem. I find them to be rather polite if you just say, "No, I don't have it, sorry." They usually don't have time to sit around and keep begging the same person for money. But that logic only worked for me in Bed-Stuy; these East New York stragglers were persistent. It wasn't so much that they begged more but that they were more insistent on not being so easily dismissed.

I was about a block away from Aaron's when I turned a corner and was approached by a haggard man. He walked up to me decisively, wearing a tattered black trench coat with a wool sweater beneath and brown pants full of stains. He did not have an odor, which was my primary concern as he invaded my personal space before catching himself and backing up a bit out of courtesy. He had an untrimmed beard and yellow eyes, though I admit he did not possess the usual delirious look of defeat so common among street people. He addressed me with the greatest poise.

"Excuse me, young brother, now look now, look…I don't mean to bother you in the least. I can see from how you dressed right now that you got very important things to get to, so I don't want to keep you for too long, I don't want to take up too much of your time, but the Lord put something on my heart to share with you. And I'm gone say too that I'm not out here on nobody's drugs or out here begging nobody for anything, I believe a strong and able-bodied man should work for his food and work for his money, it builds character, and *character* is something that a lot of all these young brothers don't have no more, because they've tried to *extinguish* all that good character out of our community. Let me be one hundred percent honest with you and say right now, though, that I *am* an alcoholic, but I don't touch no crack or heroin, and I'm not anybody's criminal. Like I said, the Lord put it on my heart to come up and share something with you, and I think it would be to your benefit if you listened to this good word."

I stood and listened, not out of a sense of curiosity but because walking away would mean I was a terrible person, cut from the same cloth as someone like Marcelle. If Contessa were watching and I walked away, she'd be ashamed, maybe even disgusted by my lack of empathy. I had to be the man she deserved.

"Now, check this out, you might find it hard to believe looking at the way I look right now, but there was once a time, not too long ago, when I had it going on just like you, but at that time I *was* using drugs and living in sin, and I allowed those things to come in and take over my life. I was an abuser and a user, you understand what I'm saying? I'm going to show you my wallet just so you know that I'm telling the truth, I ain't trying to run no game on nobody. Here we go, see that? That's my expired driver's license from 2012, and if you look closely you can also see that I used to live on the Upper West Side. I was well-to-do, I made money, I was a professor, I had a good life with a beautiful wife and three smart and beautiful children. I was living the good life for about nine years until them drugs got inside me and tore me away from my family. My wife left me, and she took the kids with her, and I ain't seen none of them for the last, what, five years? And look at this, this is my American Express card. It has my name: 'Thomas Cooper.' That's to prove that I didn't steal this wallet. All of the contents, including the three dollars inside, belong to me."

Motivated by my lack of protest, he rambled on, "I'm sure you're probably still asking yourself, 'What the hell does this old fool want?' But I assure you that I'm just trying to share my testimony with you, young brother. Now, do you know what the word *acclimate* means? To become *acclimated* to something means to become *accustomed* to, or, better yet, *used to* something, so you could say that I became *acclimated* to my lifestyle on the Upper West Side. You know for a long time I didn't eat any meat? No pork, no ham, no beef, no chicken, no veal, no turkey, no flesh, because I was eating the best, the freshest vegetables. I was eating that stuff every day, and I felt so good in the morning and so healthy and just fresh inside.

"Now, you would think with all of that going on for me, that I liked to date white women, but no, no, no, my wife was black, real black, you know what I mean, because she was from Georgia, and darker than me. Stay away from them white women, young brother. Even though they love smart brothers like you and me, do your best to stay away from them, because they don't want nothing but those African nuts, and once they get them, well, what do you think happens to a man, to an *African* man, when he loses his nuts? Think about that, young brother. Think about that, young king."

He paused to take a breath and then continued, "I know I went on for a while, but I had to speak to you out of love and concern for you because we are brothers, and I wish you all the best success on your path, and I only ask that you bless me if you can. I'm very hungry this evening, and if you can find it in your heart to help me out with anything just so I could get a sandwich to eat tonight..."

Without any delay I went for my wallet, only to be reminded again that it was empty. I searched through my other pockets, hoping desperately to find a few quarters to help the old man. His story, even if it was just a scam, had touched me. The only coins I had were those I needed to take the bus back home after leaving Aaron's—there was no way I could walk. There was nothing in my pockets, so I had to tell him that I couldn't help. He didn't miss a beat. The old man simply waved another blessing at me and bid me farewell. When I looked back after him, he had already turned the corner and disappeared into the night.

I was finally at the entrance to the housing project where Aaron lived. The Montgomery Houses was a vast collection of brick cages that had seemingly burst forth from their graves, surrounded by dead trees and garbage. The buildings looked frightening from the ground as you walked up; everything was dark, and it took a moment to realize that the blacked-out holes dotting the exterior were actually windows to apartments with people living inside. There were a couple of playgrounds with brand-new equipment, empty because of the cold. People stood outside the entrances to some of the buildings, carrying on conversations about the upcoming election or silently dragging on menthol cigarettes. Trash bags had been piled up in clumps against the iron gates; a detached kitchen sink and counter was abandoned in the middle of one of the walkways.

After some assistance with the door, I found myself in the flickering lights of the hallway. A man in a wheelchair had fallen asleep waiting on one of the two unreliable elevators. When the elevator crashed into place and ripped open, I stepped inside over a puddle of piss and pressed the button for the ninth floor. On the way up, I looked at Contessa's new profile pictures. She was still gorgeous, although she was fully covered in winter clothes now. Her hair was still billowing and full of life. I thought about the little flower she wore the night we danced together, and then the doors opened. I took a big step again so as not to step in the piss, which I had almost forgotten about, and I rang the bell at 9E.

I felt very manly when I walked in the door to Ms. Greene's apartment. She was older than me, of course, maybe in her forties, but she always welcomed me every time as if I were a father coming home to his family after a long day in the city. She would smile at me with pretty teeth, making the lines on her face vanish for just a moment. She would usher me into the living room, where a comfortable seat waited along with a glass of water and maybe even a bowl of soup. The children were in the back rooms, hidden. She always wore something loose-fitting so as not to give off the wrong impression, but her strut was impressive, and she moved about the small, dim apartment with grace, welcoming me to my seat before she yelled for Aaron to join me at the table.

"Aaron, come on, Mr. Bellinger is here," she said before turning back to me and smiling.

There was always music playing when I arrived. This time she played a song I had never heard by Mary J. Blige. The music was too loud, and, noticing my raised eyebrows, she lowered the volume, so that the sound gave way to the music playing in the back of the apartment. The smell of fried shrimp reached me before the lyrics from Aaron's room did, but eventually I made out the words.

It ain't nothing to chop that bitch off
It ain't nothing to chop that bitch off
Stupid bitch be on the nuts tho'
Crazy hoe be trying to front tho'
I bust that nut and then I'm gone tho'
Stupid hoe be like 'don't go'

Silent embarrassment washed over me after hearing those lyrics from the back room, which the highly perceptive and dutiful Ms. Greene picked up on immediately. I wasn't embarrassed for myself, having heard the song hundreds of times from passing cars outside my bedroom window. I was embarrassed for Ms. Greene. She went to great pains to give me the impression that her household was a stable and sustainable one for Aaron to study and remain drug-free in. It's true, I never smelled marijuana when I came to their apartment, but it wouldn't have been out of the ordinary from what I usually saw in most of the apartments I visited. Some of the other parents had boyfriends who wouldn't even bother to turn down the television or put out the blunt, let alone acknowledge my presence. The mothers, always a bit ashamed of their boyfriends' behavior, would smile graciously and guide me to a quieter, more hidden part of the apartment to begin working with the delinquent student. I was always able to tell how often a man stayed in the apartment by how filthy it looked.

Ms. Greene's was a clean apartment, but it was cramped, and the presence of a lurking twenty-year-old son only made it feel more suffocating. The daughter, who was not home, had begun having her boyfriend visit so often that he was becoming a member of the household. Still, it was always a relief to cross the threshold at Ms. Greene's.

As for the obscene music, I had to be honest with myself that it wasn't embarrassment that I felt for Ms. Greene after all; it was really only a small surprise, something akin to the feeling we get when someone shows up with an unexpected but useless gift, which we take with a rush of gratitude, only to place it beside a similar gift that we had received only yesterday. I hadn't expected to hear those lyrics, but I shouldn't have expected much else. The fact that Aaron's choice was such a ratchet song has no bearing on the original problem, which is the loss of silence, not merely the foul language or pornographic content that replaces that silence. After all, at twenty, Aaron was an adult and was entitled to listen to whatever he liked.

The music flowing from Aaron Greene's bedroom was, at best, unadulterated nonsense—nothing but cyclical, elementary ignorance designed to captivate the dumb and entice the feeble, and, what's more, it represented a cloaked attack on the black race in particular, in the form of hypnosis and mass entertainment, subterfuge involving the tom-tom, an irresistible beat, and a hypnotic base where vulgar lyrics turned to static.

"Boy, turn that stupid mess off, Mr. Bell is here for you!" Ms. Greene yelled out, and, just as quickly, the music was muted. Aaron came out shyly to the kitchen table, where I was sitting with his file open in front of me.

"Good evening, Mr. Bellinger," he said, taking a seat reluctantly across from me.

After we exchanged greetings, I looked down at our progress sheet to see what we might be able to finish during the session. I also wanted to see Contessa badly. The sheet indicated that it was time for me to give Aaron his piss cup for the drug test he was supposed to take in the next few days, but I had lost that some weeks ago. There was also a math assessment that he was due to take. Luckily, I did have a copy of that. As I gathered the necessary forms, Aaron sat there uninterested. His face radiated annoyance when he looked at the sheet of math problems.

"Now, you remember the last time I was here, I gave you that English assessment," I began ceremoniously. It was important not to let the GED students feel too friendly with the caseworker. "This time, I want you to do another one, except it will be in math."

"Nah, son, I don't fuck with math," he said plainly, pushing the test sheet back toward me.

"Watch your damn mouth, E!" said Ms. Greene with concern.

"It's just an assessment to help you get ready for the GED test," I went on carefully. "You've got to be prepared, or else you'll have to stay in this program and keep trying to take the test over and over."

"What kind of math is it?" He pulled the worksheet back and examined it with his mouth hanging open, frowning. "Yo, can you just take it for me, since it's not even the real test? These questions look too hard for me anyway. I'm not at that level."

"If I took the test for you, that would defeat the purpose of assessing you to see where you need help," I said, trying to maintain an air of authority.

"And I'm telling you right now, mistah, I can't do none of this. Them question look hard as shit, yo. I can't pass that."

"It's not about passing or—"

"So you saying I can fail?"

I said yes before realizing the trap he had set. When he gave the assessment back to me five minutes later, I saw that he had filled in "A" for all fifty of the multiple-choice questions. He hadn't tried to work through any of the problems; the instructions were to "add and subtract positive and negative integers." It was still my responsibility to grade the assessment, and, because he had not taken the test seriously, I basically ended up having to take it for him to do that. A large part of me wanted to say, Fine then, you dumb little nigga, and tear the test to shreds, but it would have broken poor Ms. Greene's heart. She was standing near the stove looking at Aaron and me with so much pride. Her boy was finally getting his act together, finally getting serious about life.

Aaron Greene scored a 17 percent on the assessment. I smiled at Ms. Greene with spurious goodwill when I shook her hand goodbye. The next day, I called Rosa and told her to drop the Greenes from my roster. I didn't see any of them ever again. I didn't owe anyone anything, and not even the possible disapproval of my Contessa could make me change my mind.

Chapter Seven

NOVEMBER FINALLY GAVE WAY TO DECEMBER, AND I TOOK THE TRANSITION IN STRIDE. IT WAS the fifth year in a row that I would spend Thanksgiving alone. I wasn't big on holidays. My relationship with my family back in Virginia was strained, to put it gently. You might even say that I grew up all alone, in my own head, and although I have siblings—one younger sister and an older sister who is now in prison for murder— we never were very close. My parents separated while I was in high school, mainly because my father was an alcoholic and a philanderer, but my mother was no saint either. She chased other men because she never fully respected my father, who spent the little money he did have on drinking and taking out other women. My gift to myself was being accepted to college and leaving that life behind. I hadn't returned home to Virginia in two years and probably wouldn't go back until someone died. Suffice it to say that the torture and despair I experienced growing up would make for a fine book.

December opened with a few brilliant days of sun. On the first Friday of the month, I received an invitation to attend a panel discussion and opening night at the Brooklyn Institute of Fine Art. The artist Theodore Mdembe was presenting a new work that promised to be more titillating and controversial than anything he had done before, including his most recent show, which featured the artist placing himself inside a ten-by-ten-foot steel cage in the middle of a London museum and living there, naked, for a whole two months. The Internet went into hysterics when it was discovered that Mdembe wanted nothing more than bowls for food and water and a metal pan to be used as a bathroom. All three were cleaned as often as possible. Although he was only on display for four hours a day, the artist chose to remain in the cage even after the museum closed. The show was a humongous success and was touted as the most provocative statement on race in the twenty-first century, surpassing even Kara Walker's "Sugar Mammy Sphinx," which had been erected in an abandoned sugar factory on the Brooklyn waterfront just a couple of years before.

I accepted the invitation without question. I'd always considered myself a great lover of the arts and had been to one of Mdembe's shows before, in Chicago, where he managed to perform a tap dance routine, nonstop, for twelve hours. The show was given the same amount of praise as the one in London, but a segment of reviewers thought it the work of nothing more than an art house sell out, a submissive minstrel player. As for me, I was conflicted; the performance was beautiful, the skill involved superb—he did tap dance for twelve hours. According to the artist himself, the point of all his work was "to amuse and enrage, to seduce the audience into ignoring their politically correct thinking for a moment before finally realizing that they were committing the same crime as the racists they'd been taught to despise."

I purchased one ticket and then went about getting an outfit together for the next night. I kept it plain: faded blue jeans, brown boots, a dark green wool shirt, and a heavy coat with matching scarf and gloves. I put some cash in a small envelope and slid it under Randall's door upstairs. Next I made myself a small bowl of canned chili, which I ate along with an apple and a glass of tap water. During my meal, I looked at pictures of Contessa; she'd added one new picture of her holding a cat that probably belonged to one of her girlfriends. She was still stunning, but she was clutching the cat like someone who didn't have anyone to share a laugh with before she went to bed. Maybe I was just reading too much into it. What good is it not to have innocent fantasies about the people we want? It's just a harmless daydream, although sometimes those daydreams became so vivid and sumptuous that I got nervous and had to stop looking at her pictures altogether. In such cases, when the savory memory of Contessa became unbearable, I'd let it all vanish and retreat back to the mundane reality of my computer desk.

The best remedy to neutralize those kinds of thoughts, I've found, is to look at the pictures of people I care very little about. I closed the window with Contessa's pictures, went to Instagram on my phone, and searched for the hashtag #mdembeBIFA. Seventeen people had already posted screenshots of their ticket purchases, followed by such captions as "so ready for this"; "its going to b totally epic"; and "not excited about this #coonery, but a friend bought my ticket" I switched back to my feed to see if any of the people I followed had posted anything noteworthy. There was Grace Hampton, who had purchased a new dog, some sort of Chihuahua mix, with teeth that were too large for its head. There was also the spaghetti dinner, which did look appetizing, although Patrice Clark, the cook, summarily ruined the dish in the final picture by dumping Parmesan cheese over the entire bowl like some kind of fiend. I admired Chris Dalton's use of filter in his ongoing road trip project, and I also enjoyed the underground photographer Josephine Booker's explorative collection of abandoned brownstones and empty lots throughout Brooklyn and the Bronx. On Facebook, Camron Freeman was hosting a meandering debate in his timeline. The subject involved a pair of male rappers who had put out a sex tape and statement proudly embracing their homosexuality and encouraging other black celebrities to come out of the closet in similar fashion. There were eighty-seven comments, with most of the opinions in favor of the rappers' actions, though some people had the audacity to type out "they're tools of the White Man" and even "fucking nasty smh." Part of me felt the urge to get enraged and join the debate, but if I attracted the attention of anyone in the thread with a particularly witty or snide comment I would have to stay up with the conversation until the end, and I didn't have time for that. There wasn't much else of interest. I put the phone on the charger and went straight to bed.

The next morning, I was startled out of sleep by a banging sound in the hallway. I opened my door cautiously and looked out to see Randall pulling a loveseat down the stairs. There was also a small side table holding open the front door of the building. He hadn't mentioned that he was going to be moving out, but sure enough there was a big truck waiting out front with its hazard lights on, and I could see a bed already loaded inside of it. He was in a hurry as he struggled to get the loveseat to fit between the handrails. Although it came as a relief to see him taking his things out to the truck, I wondered what I would have to do about the rent. Ever since I'd moved into my room, I'd always paid my rent to Randall in cash; I never once met the actual landlord. I wasn't sure if I'd have to move out soon as well. At least I'd have the bathroom to myself for a while. I called out to Randall to find out what was going on.

"I'll tell you all about it later tonight," he said without looking at me, keeping his focus on the stubborn loveseat. "If anyone comes around here looking for me, just tell them I went out of town a few days ago."

And with that, he finally got the chair down and out of the front door. He loaded the loveseat in the back of the truck, shut the door, and sped off in the truck over a speed bump. What else could I do but wait to talk to him later that night?

The wind was starting to pick up outside, so I stayed in bed for the rest of the day until it was time to get ready for the museum. I spent the majority of the time on my phone, of course, reading mildly interesting articles and taking casual note of the various updates to my friends' profiles. I came across a blog post condemning Mdembe for being a "culture vulture" of the African American experience on account of his being a Nigerian artist who worked exclusively on subject matter related to American slavery. The post pointed out that the artist had only come to America for graduate school and thus had no real connection to the "Black American Experience." I wondered if the blogger lived in Brooklyn and whether or not she would be coming to tonight's event.

The opening was set to begin at seven o'clock, so I left the house at six, anticipating a long line to get inside. I was right; when I came up from the train at the BIFA station, the line snaked around the corner and doubled back on itself. In spite of the cold there was an absolute frenzy outside the museum. Apart from the line, a large crowd of onlookers had gathered, apparently having decided it was worth standing in the cold just to get a look at all of the people who'd actually managed to get tickets.

The museum building itself was impressive. The BIFA, housed in a neoclassical structure, sat at the triangular intersection formed by Flatbush, Atlantic, and Sixth Avenues, with its facade facing the southern approach of Flatbush. From there, I was able to see three large vertical banners hanging from the building's cornice. Each one featured a striking, if not garish, close-up of Mdembe's face. The first banner showed the artist smiling widely with his teeth clenched tightly together; the second focused exclusively on his wide eyes and raised brows; the final banner zeroed in on the artist's nose, the nostrils flared up as if the picture had been taken just before he was about to sneeze. Viewed from the avenue, with the brake lights and headlights of the bumper-to-bumper traffic, the banners gave the impression that a giant black man was inside the museum, shackled behind a curtain on a stage, waiting to be viewed by a clueless public.

The massive crowd continued to swell in size, and, in true New York fashion, the newly arrived were creating a spectacle of expensive winter coats and hats and dazzling scarves. A veritable fashion show formed near the entrance as the ticket holders arrived in cabs or from the subway station. Every variation of natural hair was to be seen on the heads of the women, from dyed locs to two-toned Afros to intricate arrangements of braids. Some of the men wore beards and fedoras, long wool coats, and leather gloves, while others sported expensive sneakers or seasonal dress shoes.

About a third of the crowd wore glasses. They all looked smart, and you could hear sophisticated opinions being shared about Mdembe's oeuvre and the nature of Black art. There were a few local celebrities attempting to look nondescript, perhaps upset that they were forced to wait in line with everyone else. The singer Joanna Knight, known for her modern take on the slave work songs, was there with an unknown woman, perhaps on a date. Chelsea Little, the digital artist highly regarded for her pixelated portraits of black vaginas, stood near me, laughing and smoking cigarettes with an adoring group of friends. Everett Benson, who had made a name for himself with a recently published memoir, was also nearby, immersed in some profane debate with two other people.

I was standing in line taking all of this in when, at 7:14, the line began to move. There must have been two hundred people ahead of me and an equal number behind me. People were starting to take pictures of themselves, their friends, and the immense banners when I saw Contessa walking right past me toward the end of the line. She was alone. She wore a marvelous burgundy overcoat with black leather gloves and boots. There was her red lipstick and blush again, and her famously spirited mane. She didn't see me as she walked by. I worried that she might be looking to meet up with Marcelle, but my instincts told me he would never come to an opening, that it was more likely that he was somewhere planning an after-party instead. It took every drop of reserve to keep myself from calling out to Contessa and offering her a place in line. That would have been too overt and thirsty. I needed to make the best of this opportunity.

The line lurched forward at a constant pace, and soon enough I was able to see the ticket scanners at the entrance. It was my first time dealing with them, but I watched as other people went in without pulling out their phones to show their tickets; the little machine scanned it off of your phone even if it was in your pocket. I thought that was very convenient. Once inside, I followed the people ahead of me to another set of doors where about fifty of us had to stand and wait for a short time. Everyone was excited. Finally, an official opened the doors and motioned us to enter.

The gallery space turned out to be a vast hall, maybe three hundred feet wide and five hundred feet long, with a ceiling some thirty stories above. The entire space was filled with man-made trees and grass, taking on the look of a lush forest. The intricacy and detail of the trees was astonishing, each being carved with great care, the trunks and branches looking naturally twisted, gnarled more so by the passage of many seasons than by the painstaking labor of the artist. An artificial stream offered glittering water bounded by a dreamlike array of flowers in various and vivid colors. A mesmerizing assortment of papier-mâché butterflies sat amid the flowers and the ceiling, and the walls had been painted to resemble a soft purple evening sky. It was as if we had come across an undiscovered enchanted forest.

For a brief moment, you would have thought we had entered a veritable paradise, complete with boulders to explore, until you noticed the black bodies hanging from some of the branches, some of them burned and others of them "fresh" except for the little streams of artificial blood running down the exposed chests, backs, and legs. The artist seemed to have taken even greater care in rendering the facial expressions of the would-be corpses than he had in the details of the trees; each face was contorted with pain and bewilderment, a few even featured swollen tongues jutting out of their mouths. There must have been about twenty "bodies" representing men and women with their genitals in full view, either attached or in the grass just beneath them. The entire setting was a fusion of fantasy and nightmare, and it soon struck me with the qualities of an insane hallucination. I was dumbfounded. Some of the spectators actually turned to leave, but the more adventurous went ahead and touched the bodies, surprised that they actually swung.

I realized then that a great amount of time had passed since I'd felt genuinely stunned by something. If I take the moment that Contessa first called out my name on the train as the highest and most paralyzing degree of amazement I'd ever felt, this came to approach that feeling, but it did not surpass it. In that first encounter with Contessa, the affair was intoxicating but private; the other passengers in the train car had no notion of the sudden warmth that rushed over me. They didn't notice the pride and the succulent tension that builds after being recognized in a crowd. Little moments like that, the brief rush of joy and alarm we get to experience without ever calling attention to ourselves, are remarkable because we feel immediately changed without anyone else being the wiser. But to walk into a gallery of lynching, now, that was altogether embarrassing—not because I felt any particular shame at having to look at such a vicious portrayal of history, but because it was clear that I was at a loss for how to account for what I was viewing, just like everyone else. We were collectively stupefied, and although it's true that some reacted by touching the bodies admiringly or else by taking pictures and smiling the way people used to do in those old lynching postcards, I was willing to wager that no one really knew what to make of the scene; they were just better than me at hiding it.

I caught sight of Contessa just as a small group of people were moving on from spinning one of the bodies. She stopped the body from swinging and moved in closer to examine the feet. She was still alone. I walked right up to her.

"Hi, Simone? What's up? Is Marcelle here, too?" I had to get the formalities out of the way.

She looked at me quizzically for a second, then recognized me. "Oh, hi, Adrian!" She smiled and opened her arms to hug me. I wanted to hold on to her for longer, naturally, but I kept my composure and stepped back a little. "Yeah, um, Marcelle didn't want to come. He hates Mdembe. I didn't know you were into him?"

"Me? Oh, yes! I've been into his work for years. I saw his last big show in Chicago, and I thought it was amazing." I was happy to have found some common ground.

Apparently, the shocking display of lynched bodies did nothing to disturb Contessa. She was smiling, freely touching the feet and examining the streams of blood as if they were dresses for sale in a department store. She had no reservations whatsoever, though this could have been an act to hide her confusion. Then again, she looked entirely dedicated to those bloodied feet; she displayed a morbid side that I hadn't been able to glean from any of her social media.

"He's been working on these cadavers for three years," she said. "There's a total of fifteen of them in this exhibit, and each one contains a full model skeleton inside. He said he based the faces of each body on his own family members. The ambition in the corpses alone shows his mastery of sculpture, to say nothing of the surrounding forest."

I nodded in agreement, desperately hoping that her admiration ended with the work and did not extend to the artist himself. Just the same, I was now willing to read every book about Mdembe so that I could always have something to talk to Contessa about. It seemed that as long as I was able to stand and listen, I would get to be next to her all evening.

"I think, on the whole, the piece isn't even about slavery or Jim Crow, or at least it's about something even deeper than the two. He's managed to get a diverse group of people to contemplate a brutal era in American history, that's certainly true, but he's also managed to make it beautiful, and that's the genius of it. He's taken the whole 'We Shall Overcome' bullshit and made it gorgeous instead of just pitiful.

"It's got the same mystical, eerie quality as Doris Ulman's 'Baptism in the River,' especially with regard to the construction of the forest setting, but there's also an element of Aaron Douglas's silhouettes in his 'Harriet Tubman' mural, and also take note of the bodies, which borrow so tastefully from Eldzier Cortor's nudes, and though it's all so serene, it's captured that same frenzy of movement found in Barnes's 'Sugar Shack,' as if the bodies were dancing in their nooses."

I hadn't realized she was such a well of knowledge. Did Marcelle appreciate her boundless mind?

"Now turn this way," she said, taking me by the shoulder, "and you can see how he even put little paintings on some of the leaves. They're a bit hard to see from a distance, but those are adinkra symbols stamped on the undersides of the leaves. The symbol means *mmere dane*, or 'life changes' ...

"I'm also really impressed that he chose to stay away from the silhouette method and instead camouflage the bodies against the backdrop of the forest; it adds to the unsettling experience of walking into a paradise, only to realize it's actually a kind of hell. The use of natural colors for the skin lets us know that the victims were real people—young individuals, at that. I'm almost certain that if we could reach up to the eyelids and pull them back, we would find that only some of them have brown eyes. I mean, look at that one—it's light-skinned with reddish hair and freckles. And look at the teeth on this one, some of them are missing. If only we could get closer to the hair ..."

Contessa moved around the gallery with the comfort of a coroner in a morgue coupled with the jubilance of a child surrounded by new presents, stopping to examine one before being pulled away by yet another charm beside it. She was absolutely serious about her analysis of the work, and this confirmed my hypothesis that if she wasn't a photographer, she was definitely immersed in the arts. I also couldn't help but feel that it wasn't me she was talking to at all, but to some invisible pupil following her around taking hurried notes for an upcoming exam. At times she would go on talking even when her back was turned to me. I wanted to take her by the arm and tell her not to forget about me, her only true friend in the building, but I quickly scrubbed the thought from my mind because she was so naturally impressive as a speaker and I didn't want to interrupt her. She was all graceful movement; she had been well-balanced the night of the dance, but here she was in her element. She was careful not to trample any of the plants as some of the other patrons had done. After examining a body, she would stop it from swinging and allow it to settle before she moved on. What had begun as a macabre lecture in this cemetery of sorts was slowly turning into a guided tour though the brain of Contessa. This encounter greatly exceeded our dance at the party. Back then I felt out of sync with her. There was no real way for us to hold a conversation with all of the music and rowdiness, and it was so dark that I really couldn't see her face clearly. Here, we were looking at corpses together, talking about art together—though, I admit, she did most of the talking—and just being seen out together.

A photographer, a good-looking woman whom I recognized from Facebook, walked up to the two of us and said that we made such a cute and well-dressed couple that we should pose together. This sudden good fortune made me stiff until Contessa, not showing any hesitation at the opportunity, pulled me beside her and smiled. Just like that, there was a flash, and Contessa and I were together forever—somewhere on the Internet.

With that, the gray despair that first settled over me the night I learned that Marcelle and Contessa were an item evaporated entirely. I felt reinvigorated, like an anxious gladiator back in his arena with his spear after months of recuperation and training. I was aware again of the great beauty and good fortune of being alive after enduring defeat in a little skirmish. Sometimes, it really is better to retreat for a while so as not to be completely decimated in battle. Retreat and study the habits of the target, then attack once more.

This surge in confidence was the result of a new realization that had come to me after so many weeks stuck in conjecture and speculation. Before the art show, I had gleaned most of my ideas about Contessa from the pictures on her page, but this was really a terrible mistake, seeing as how her pictures created the impression of an average woman with average interests. All of those pictures taken with family members, ex-boyfriends, and celebrities in nightclubs acted like a shield hiding the real Contessa, who was not only a high-minded art enthusiast but also just as elegant as I had originally thought she would be before I found her online. In person, she always struck me as regal. Online, she seemed ordinary, and the gaps in our physical contact were filled with online memories that obscured the actual Contessa. So there was the old problem resurfacing again, of too much time being spent online looking at people who I should simply talk to in person. But, in my situation, it would have to do. I wasn't yet able to see Contessa at will, nor had I gone so far as to ask for her number. This small problem would have to be remedied somehow, and soon; I couldn't stand the thought of retreating again back to my phone to look at her pictures without first setting up another meeting in the near future.

There was also the idea that, if Contessa had enough sensibility to have a discerning eye for art, it could be wagered she was sensitive enough to have picked up on my feelings for her from the very beginning, prompting her to call out my name on the train as a way of winking at me. But without solid confirmation of this, I risked creating a disaster, so I resolved that before the night came to an end I would ask Contessa once and for all, not, "*How* did you know my name?" but "*Why* did you say my name?" The question would be forward enough to tear away the lingering haziness regarding any mutual feelings but subtle enough to remain draped in innocence, staving off the possibility of being labeled an advance.

The plan made me ecstatic, and I congratulated myself for having worked through it so ingeniously as I followed Contessa through the gallery. "Hold on a minute, Simone." I interrupted her just as she was beginning to discuss Mdembe's underdeveloped chiaroscuro in some of his earlier paintings. "I want you to tell me more about this relationship between Mdembe and Rembrandt, but do you think we could get some water and sit down for a bit?"

"Oh, sure! I know I was going on and on, right?" She smiled, finally seeing the rest of the world around her.

We walked out of the exhibit together like a couple; the other patrons still waiting in line eyed us as such. I knew that gossip was already spreading like a stain through the entire museum. Of course, not everyone knew who we were, but certainly a few of the visitors did, and no doubt they were typing shady texts to their friends about seeing Addy and Simone, or maybe taking sneaky snapshots or snickering with their friends and pointing. I remembered Tracy's earlier assumption that I had a crush on the DJ at her party; at least now people would get the gender right.

When we came to the water fountains, Contessa said that she needed to use the restroom. After my drink, I composed myself for the question I wanted to as. If Contessa did indeed harbor romantic feelings for me, I would be naive to expect that she would come right out and express them in the lobby, but I would pay close attention to the slightest changes in her face and posture. Any quick tightening of the jaw or sudden raising of her brows would be enough. Or would she pretend not to remember the day altogether? She might say something about Marcelle mentioning me in passing. I doubt that she would admit to stalking me on my profile page, although it was very likely she had.

I put a tremendous amount of effort into curating my page. I posted one selfie and one picture from college weekly. I only allowed tagged pictures if women took them or if I was posing in the picture with conventionally attractive women. Whenever I visited the Rockaways I made sure that the picture I took was positioned from such an angle that I could lie about the location and give off the illusion of an exotic tropical escape. I'd post one picture of me at Jones Beach followed by a bunch of stock photos of Rio, pictures of markets and old architecture and the like, creating the impression that I had visited South America. Of course, no one cared to check and see if I was telling the truth, because the truth doesn't matter; it's all about how you make a person feel when they come to your page. Pictures of exotic flowers, crumbling cathedrals, good-looking women with great hair and pretty shoes—those things make people happy and nostalgic and horny, and that's really what life is all about these days. I think I have about thirteen hundred friends; most of them were lured in because of my talent for creating a spectacle on my profile page.

Curiously, even if she had visited my page, Contessa hadn't sent me a friend request. I took that as a bit of an insult, although it was probably for the best. Contessa's page was no doubt curated as well; she was definitely hiding the fact that she was a nerd. That's just the way it is. You need to tell little lies or hold back the real you so that you have something to talk about in person because everybody knows everything about everybody else. Obviously, Contessa understood this.

She came out of the hallway that the restrooms were in and stopped to look at her phone. I was going to get to the heart of things, and to chill myself out I took a seat on a nearby bench. That's when I saw him, sifting through the crowd of patrons just like he had in the subway. He wore the same mischievous grin, as if he had heard everything about my plot and was coming over to gloat on his timely intrusion.

"What's going on, you ugly ass nigga? Where you been at?" He gripped me into a hug, smiling widely.

"Working most of the time. This is like the first time I've really been out in a while," I said, deflated.

He surveyed the hall, then said, "Well, what you getting into tonight? I know Simone is up here. Have you seen her?"

"Yeah, we spoke earlier. She's over there by the bathrooms."

"Damn, I got to deal with her now. I thought she would've already left."

"Did you see the exhibit?" I asked.

Marcelle turned to me proudly, "Oh, yes, nigga, the video been going around online for a cool minute, but I ain't got time for that spooky haunted house shit right now. Mdembe a fool for this one though."

"Yeah, but the video can't really stand up to the real thing..."

"Nigga, did you see the video? It was like two hours long, going in on how this fool got the hair for the bodies' heads from real barbershops in Bed-Stuy."

That was a detail the placards for the exhibit had failed to mention.

"We getting ready to go to the after-party for it, though. You trying to come, too?"

It was out of the question that I would make myself the third wheel. At that point I just wanted to go home and look through my phone. If I had taken Marcelle up on his offer, it would have meant standing around for hours as the enemy basked in his victory. I'd heard the sneaky rhythm of insinuation in his voice. No doubt there would be kissing and hand-holding, but, even worse, there might be cuddling and whispering, forcing me to stand there like a child who'd dropped his ice cream cone. They would make me play the supporting friend role in this tactical assault of Marcelle's, and it might mean Contessa became convinced of my strictly platonic feelings for her. I could not let Marcelle gain that kind of ground so easily, with so little effort, reveling in victory even as the battle was being fought.

Contessa came over to join us, and Marcelle pulled her in for a kiss. I'd never seen them do that before.

"So you coming, Addy? You know it's gone be some women there," he said, rubbing his chin after the kiss.

That too was another tactic of his, mentioning that there would be women there, knowing my refusal would go just that much further in making me look like a downer to Contessa.

I smiled irreverently and backed away from the bait. It was time to get away from them at that point. No point in extending an embarrassing episode.

There's only so much time a man has before he gets trapped in that purgatory of romance: the friend zone. If you're not overt enough in the pursuit, you may as well disappear altogether. Otherwise you risk being seen as a good guy. I probably shouldn't have even said one word to Contessa. Now she had probably filed me away as a dud or an awkward acquaintance of Marcelle's. I felt the trench between us widening. My mistake? Shyness. There was nothing wrong with going up to a woman you really loved and announcing it then and there. And what was so terrible about that, even if her boyfriend was around? Couldn't she see that Marcelle was slick and disrespectful? He didn't even care that she was at the museum.

I reconsidered the offer briefly; the opportunity might come for me to best Marcelle in conversation in front of Contessa. But he wasn't going to play by the rules. He'd somehow inject well-timed vulgarity into things, knowing I wouldn't be willing to stay in that kind of conversation. He would use his vulgarity to get free rein over the topic at hand. Marcelle was willing to sling mud.

"I'm meeting up with somebody a little later," I said, trying to remain coolheaded.

"Oh, you got a new girl now?"

"No, just a friend."

"Well, all right then, handle that, my nigga."

Cordially, I reached in to hug Contessa with one arm, and then I did the same with Marcelle. We parted ways. Contessa's scent was still embedded in my coat when the train hissed into place in front of me on the platform. It was almost ten o'clock, and the train was full of people ending their nights early. The lights on board flickered, then went out completely for a few minutes. It would have been completely dark were it not for the dozens of phone screens that let out a conjuring, soothing glow throughout the train car. You could see the soft blue light rendering the faces. Everyone was concentrating on swiping or watching videos. When the real lights returned, no one looked up. They were all still looking down at their screens when I got off at my stop.

I ordered a greasy sandwich from a pizza place across the street from the station. There was turkey and old lettuce with mustard squirted in between to cover up the taste of stale bread. I was hungry, though, and this was a solution. I came out of the pizza shop and gave some change to a haggard old woman who was crying about not having any shoes. The night promised a creeping snowstorm. Some flakes were already falling and settling into various nooks: on top of side-view mirrors, near the curbs, on people's shoulders. Without an umbrella, my ears were getting wet. I walked faster, squeezing by a doting couple with Whole Foods bags. I was jealous of their intimacy.

When I made it within sight of my building, I saw a crowd of people enduring the cold to look up my stairwell. There was an ambulance outside with its lights popping and rolling, casting a purple glow on the buildings. As I made it closer, I heard my neighbor, Mr. Barkley, saying he knew it was gunshots because he'd been in Vietnam. There were still more people choking the stairs when a police car pulled up and parked out front. The two officers jumped out of the car and scurried up the steps, clearing a path for the stretcher. They came outside with Randall's lifeless body under a sheet that covered everything but his face. People drew back, gasping, but when the stretcher was right in front of me, I pulled out my phone and took a picture without even thinking.

Chapter Eight

I NEVER THOUGHT TO COUNT RANDALL AS A FRIEND UNTIL I SAW HIM DEAD. THERE WAS nothing for me to do with the picture except look at it and keep it to myself. I didn't know how long I would keep it in my phone. I wasn't going to put it on the Internet. Perhaps I could have showed it to Randall's parents, but they weren't around, and I figured it would be especially cruel seeing as how they didn't even know me. I gazed at Randall's face on the screen, which was more comfortable to look at than his actual face and body on the stretcher, and then I put my phone away. His expression was not unlike the ones I'd just seen at the museum. Mdembe was accurate.

Randall and I were not friends in the truest sense, but I knew a few things about him on account of us living together. He was born in Brooklyn and was in his early forties by the time I met him. He had been unemployed for about two years after being caught stealing on the job; he worked at a specialty coffee shop in the Village and took his liberties with pounds of coffee beans, which he would later sell to a smaller shop in Bed-Stuy. When he told me the story one evening, we both laughed about it. After losing that job, he earned money under the table helping his uncle break locks in storage facilities. Whenever a customer fell too far behind on their storage fees, Randall and his uncle were called in to haul away the furniture and boxes. Most often, they would sell the goods online or just hold a stoop sale, but sometimes Randall would keep things. Two years of this hoarding had rendered one of the rooms in our apartment unlivable, being packed tightly with boxes of party supplies, golf clubs, old dress shoes, a variety of folding chairs, two small novelty chalkboards, an old car bumper, Christmas lights, three milk crates filled with Nintendo video game cartridges, and, his most prized finding of all, five cardboard boxes full of hip-hop and R&B cassette tapes from the 1980s and 90s. The tapes sat in the room for about a week until he came home one day with an old boom box with a dual cassette player. From then on, Randall played the music continuously, and this was initially a very welcome occurrence. I had never been into music; I didn't download it or stream it. Growing up, my household was devoid of music; my parents never played CDs, and without cable TV there was no real way to see all of the great music videos that were coming out. In college, I had to fall mute whenever the topic of the greatest musician or singer came up.

Of course I knew about Michael Jackson, the Beatles, and James Brown, but having never developed a taste for much else, I glossed over music entirely. By the time I was old enough to party, I felt that most of the music was too vulgar, and I had no motivation to go back and search for the classics once downloading had come into vogue. But Randall, who had been born in the seventies, came of age in the glorious early days of music's transformation from disco into hip-hop, from soul to R&B.

At first, I would hear something lovely playing in the living room and out of curiosity I would ask Randall who the artist was. This question always ignited him, prompting a brief listening session for the both of us wherein he would call out such titles as Vanessa Williams's "If You Really Love Him" or Wrecks-N-Effect's 1989 hit "New Jack Swing," which happened to be one of his all-time favorites. He played the track and rewound it perpetually. From there, he moved on to songs by Barbara Mason, Shalamar, and—I remember vividly—Whitney Houston's and Michael Jackson's "Take Good Care of My Heart."

Randall's music selections far surpassed just about everything I'd heard on the radio or at parties in Bed-Stuy. I like to think that this was because those old songs still believed in things like love, jealousy, heartbreak, and real joy. Their artists had the capacity to experience passion. According to Randall, the new music was basically ruined by nineties hip-hop, especially the West Coast variety. "Them cats out there was mad ignorant," he would say in complete disgust. I hadn't heard much of that music either, but I promised myself to ask Marcelle about this opinion one day. In support of Randall's view, I did notice that much of the hip-hop that I had listened to before were mere rips and samples of these cassette tape classics.

This little tidbit of a gift was Randall's one redeeming quality in my eyes: this music collection (which must have originally belonged to a DJ) and his ability to choose the right song at the right time. Otherwise, Randall was the sneaky, snooping roommate who always knew when and how much to steal from me without me noticing immediately, placing him on the level of a rat. And there was also the problem of the bathroom sink towel.

All of the signs were there from the beginning when I first came across his ad online looking for a roommate. It read, "XL room, easily fit king-size bed, w/window, for African American roommate please. Hart [*sic*] of Bed-Stuy, $600 a month." There were no pictures included in the ad, but I went in for it because it was affordable and it was in a black neighborhood. It was also only the second apartment I had the chance to look inside before settling in New York, the first being the apartment of an old college friend named David, where I slept on the couch for two weeks before meeting Randall.

When I typed in the address Randall sent me, I was annoyed by its distance from David's Harlem apartment, something like one hour that actually ended up feeling like two. In many ways, the two neighborhoods were vastly different, Harlem being just as plagued by blight and crime but also featuring a lively nightlife scene and flocks of gorgeously dressed people day and night. You could be dapper in Harlem and not feel out of place, even if you did live across the street from a fried chicken shack. There were nightclubs and restaurants that catered to black people in three-piece suits and women in mesmerizing gowns. There was a kind of high-blood-pressure energy up there, choking its way through all of the big avenues and bars and barbershops, forcing you along past parks on hills and basketball courts. And when you looked up, you saw people sitting in their windows smoking cigarettes, spitting on the oblivious pedestrians below. All of the crazy people in Harlem, generally around 125th and Lenox, had standings in the community that surpassed those of the newcomers. The lost and permanently displaced had been at their posts barefoot and unashamed for twenty years, politely asking for change or preaching or screaming at invisible phantoms, endearing themselves to the doctors, shop owners, and families who all knew that Harlem wasn't Harlem without its proud collection of lunatics and miserable junkies.

But I had to leave all of that frightening and frenzied cohesion alone and take my bags to Bed-Stuy in Brooklyn, where the staid but blemished elegance of Harlem is replaced by a kind of cosmopolitan grittiness. So on that first fearsome night when I went to look at the room for rent in Randall's two-level apartment, I was taken aback by the graffiti and action in the streets. "What world was I in?" I thought as I walked amid the impressive brownstones that seemed caught in a standoff, thousands of windows staring coldly at one another. Piles of garbage belched out from empty lots filled with overgrown mugwort. Gloomy parking lots held big voices that shouted across the concrete. But this is always the impression one has when walking into a foreign place at night for the first time.

Eventually the menacing atmosphere gave way to a quaintness that I had never felt in Harlem. Even at night, the proliferation of trees lets you know that there are peaceful, inspiring blocks in the neighborhood with its funk music and barbecue grills and so many churches. I noticed that people sitting on their stoops grew quiet when I walked by, unlike the frenetic storytellers on Harlem sidewalks who pretended never to notice me. These stoop dwellers were assessing me, but I pressed on until I made it to the apartment.

I knew from the first look at it that the room was going to be my new home. It was cheap, and I didn't want to make consecutive trips back and forth looking at other places. The room was too small for anything but a twin-sized bed, and its only window opened out into the hallway. There was a pipe in one corner that ran from the ceiling down through a hole in the floor. I imagined clouds of mice scurrying out of it. The pipe emanated thick heat throughout the room. The wooden floor was clean enough, but the walls were covered with handprints and other stains, evoking the atmosphere of a crime scene. Randall stood over my shoulder anxiously, like a used car salesman who knows the car you're looking to buy is going to break down once you put it on the highway. "It's better than the couch," I thought. I moved into the room the next day.

Most of the time, we stayed out of each other's way. I'd be leaving for work in the morning and Randall would be sitting there in a dingy robe stooped over a bowl of oatmeal watching a DVD. He'd be in the same robe watching another DVD when I came home in the evening, only the oatmeal would have been switched out for a TV dinner that smelled awful. Sometimes I would notice little pieces of meat on his plate that I'd kept in the refrigerator for myself, but I never made a fuss about it. I just tried to hide my food better the next time, though he found his way into everything eventually. Other days we'd actually chat for a while. That's how I found out what he did for money and why the apartment was so filled with junk. He spoke fondly of his job at McMillan's, the coffee shop. People always seem to have that one accomplishment that they cling to, that "good job" that, for once, made them feel like they had achieved something that was never a dream of theirs to begin with, but was still somehow just as prestigious. It lets other people know that we aren't worthless failures after all, that we haven't wasted our lives completely.

It's kind of pathetic seeing someone reminisce about a job that never gave a fuck about them, but it's still something to say to people when you want to look good and credible during an otherwise lousy and unemployed time in life. And it's not just with jobs; people do it with relationships, cars, exquisite dinners, schools, trips to exotic places—but the old "good job" always carries the worst sting, because people can tell that you actually believed, for just a moment, that it would last forever.

Sometimes it's not until the person is really gone that you have a moment to take them into consideration fully. You have to think about all of the things they did that made you laugh a little, and, if you're lucky, it can vindicate their petty crimes. I cannot say that Randall's death was a great surprise, however, because thieves are despised by everyone nowadays. Was it money that he owed? Had someone come looking for his stolen goods? I chose the Ancient Egyptian method of thinking about his thievery, wherein it was acceptable for the thief to keep a fourth of whatever he stole so long as it was all accounted for, but apparently the Brooklyn view of what Randall had done did not align with mine.

I think Contessa would have admired my leniency. I imagined her as a regal judge in one of the courts at Thebes, administering justice to Randall and I, mercifully but swiftly, her countenance and intelligence coaxing the both of us toward her higher morality. It occurred to me then that my blossoming rumination on the nature of my acquaintance with Randall had become a distraction from the more important goal at hand; namely, the development of my next and final plan of attack in the matter of Contessa and Marcelle. The very moment that I began drifting away from this history of Randall, one of the officers knocked on my door to interview me about the victim. Although I was completely innocent, I grew nauseated at the prospect of talking to any police officer whatsoever, worrying that I might be used as a scapegoat, or else that I might be blamed for some other, entirely unrelated, infraction merely on account of my being black and in proximity. The image of the dangling carcasses, my own among them, flashed into my head as I opened the door. In fact, the two officers were strangely cordial and morbidly direct. After asking where I had been and what my relation to Randall was, they left me to go and speak with some of the neighbors. I suppose I took it as a compliment that I didn't seem guilty.

After the officer finished with his questions, I didn't want to say another thing about Randall; the dead deserve their silence, their peace. To be brutally honest, I wanted nothing more than to look at Contessa online and stare at her albums to motivate myself. I did, however, transfer Randall's image from my phone to my laptop, believing it would make for a good entry one day, on one of those occasions where you and some other people are all trying to upstage one another with interesting content found on the Internet.

Later that night, while the investigators were still going over the crime scene upstairs, Contessa uploaded a picture of herself standing in the diabolical clutches of Marcelle in some bar near the museum. He was leering at the camera like a serpent or a starving jackal. He was leering at me, knowing full well that I would see the picture almost immediately. I "liked" it and went to bed.

In spite of the events of the previous night—or maybe because of them—I slept soundly and woke up refreshed and determined. My goal was clear.

Chapter Nine

THE PLOT CAME TO ME IN A DREAM, OR MAYBE IT CREPT IN BETWEEN MY EARS AFTER WAKING, but it was there before I realized it, and that was satisfying. I was more certain of myself than ever before because the plot was so deliciously simple, its success guaranteed. In fact, I had already used a version of it when I met Contessa at the party. That so much time had passed before it dawned on me to use the old approach once more confounded me. The best way to entice someone is to entice those around them. You have to inspire a little envy in people sometimes. We're all so thoroughly convinced that we should be the object of the whole world's admiration that we've taken to posting pictures of ourselves half-naked in the bathroom for the approval of our friends.

It takes a special level of vanity to show off a picture of oneself with a toilet in the background, lid and seat flipped up, or an empty tube of toothpaste in the foreground. Even more heartbreaking is the tendency of people to post such pictures without even cleaning the spit off the mirror beforehand, so anxious is their need to hoard validation from strangers. And this was a part of the special appeal of Contessa, a sweet girl who never posted one selfie. Her pictures bore the mark of authenticity, which is such a rarity in these times. They were authentic because the pictures were meaningful; all of her photos were filled with friends and family members. Not one selfie, not one image of Contessa in her pajamas or Contessa eating an ice cream cone with sunglasses on, or pointing at a monument, not even one picture of her with duck lips. I tried the expression and can say, once and for all, that it is not very comfortable.

But the plot. My plan of attack. My deceptively simple series of maneuvers. Having Contessa for myself, snatching her from the dirty paws of Marcelle finally, after so many months spent festering in cruel isolation. I was about to achieve something I felt I had waited a lifetime for, the kind of waiting that involves a profound loneliness and makes one's insides brittle. Any number of little tragedies could have befallen me, ground me into dust, before I got to have my moment with Contessa. My bones were tired of grinding against one another in the daily effort to get out of bed without having come any closer to her. I walked around with a dark pit gaping inside my chest that pushed against shriveled lungs. Breathing was a labor. My knees cracked whenever I took the stairs. Moon after moon of unbearable patience, itself a kind of remedy for the ailments it caused. Only by suffering through those nights would I be able to experience the grand release necessary to cleanse myself for Contessa. I had to be pure for her.

My idea involved befriending Marcelle like never before. I would invite him over to my apartment that very morning and let him drink as much as he pleased. He loved to be drunk. I imagined what his face would look like after he saw the liter of liquor I'd have waiting for him on my table. While drinking, I would ask for his advice and get him to speak on the most flattering topics: "How is the drug game different today compared to the nineties?" He would smile and recount embellished tales from his younger days. "How do you get a girl to be sprung off the dick? Where does Simone work?" I would take the conversation there as quickly as possible, hoping he would look her profile up on my computer. "Where does Simone live?" That was all I really needed to know.

My phone rang. Who could it be this early? It was Theresa, my boss from the drug counseling office. I picked up the phone.

"No, I don't have any visits scheduled for today. Yes, I'm interested in the family in Bensonhurst. Yes, I'm interested in two more in Bed-Stuy. Okay, just one in Bed-Stuy, the other family is in Crown Heights. Yes, that all sounds very good. I've worked there before. I'll come and pick it up this week? Okay."

I wanted every dopehead she could give me because I needed more money for Contessa. When we court women, we must have at least one of two weapons at our disposal: creativity or money. If we have both, victory is guaranteed, but creativity trumps money because cash alone, though it can dazzle and elicit a grin, can never do much for the soul, inherently mysterious and thus always in need of a kind of nourishment that can't be bought.

I accepted the new clients that Theresa offered and hung up the phone. I would have to visit the Bensonhurst family the next day. Until then, I'd start the ball rolling and send Marcelle a text inviting him over for drinks.

> came across a bottle
> of wild turkey. thinking
> about quitting job. wanna
> get drunk?

My message was off, and it gave me a curious, soothing feeling to know that Marcelle was reading it just then. The ultimate surprise: an invitation to get drunk on someone else's dime.

The snow was still falling outside, and a resolute quiet had settled over the streets. For once, there was no music in the apartment, and I admit the world feels a little different, a little more cruel, when your regularly scheduled Janet Jackson tracks fail to come wafting in under your door, urging you to dance when the mood calls for reverie and depression. It makes you wonder how much more sinister America is going to be when they finally manage to get rid of music entirely.

Marcelle replied, you want me to drink you under the table i see. What the address? Home now?

Ha yeah right!! and I sent him the address. I still needed to get this fabled bottle of Wild Turkey, so I dressed in a hurry, taking no small delight in removing Randall's bathroom sink towel for the last time. I tossed the stained and faded rag in the trash can, and as the lid closed I considered its slam to be a true symbol of the next phase of my life. The post-Randall era was now beginning.

On my way to the store, boots crunching in the fresh layer of snow, I turned over the strategy in my head, wondering which questions would be best suited to disarming Marcelle and finding out everything I needed to know about Contessa. It was true that Marcelle was crafty, but he was not methodical; he wasn't one to be held at bay by any sort of planning. I would have to use this fact to my advantage. I had already done so by sending him the text about drinking out of the blue. As for the question of whether or not I was taking advantage of an alcoholic, the answer was no. Although he rarely turned down a drink, alcohol was not his true poison. If I really needed to compromise his integrity, I could have introduced him to some nubile beauty who frequented one of the neighborhood parties, but it was never my intention to discredit or ruin Marcelle. I only wanted something I knew he was incapable of appreciating, and therefore something that might bring about his demise. My actions were helpful— springing from my own carnal desires, that was true, but from desires nevertheless wedded to charity and a deep, heartfelt concern for harmony and order.

Even with the snowfall, the neighborhood winos were already in position. The freezing cold did nothing to clear them from standing at the entrance to the liquor store. Their presence made my own questionable; by association, I was, at least for the moment, a desperate wino, too. Another unearned and minor victory for Marcelle, who wouldn't have to be seen going inside such a filthy liquor store this early in the day, whereas when the inevitable rumor finished its first cycle around the neighborhood it would be common knowledge that Adrian was a complete drunk. "Let them have it!" I thought.

As I approached the door, the winos seemed to huddle even closer to it as if to block me from entering altogether. I knew this maneuver well as the opening movement of the panhandle, a collective one, no less. I got closer, and at the last possible second one of the drunks opened the door for me, held out his ashy, ungloved hand, and asked for a dollar, which I promptly gave him, considering that I hadn't been bothered by any begging all week. This charitable act had the effect of robbing the other winos of the will to beg; they knew that one handout was the best they could expect.

Inside the store I scanned the shelves for Wild Turkey, which I knew Marcelle would enjoy because he always spoke highly of overproof liquor. I was sort of worried because I was not a heavy drinker whatsoever. When the lightweights try to keep up with the heavyweights, terrible forces work together to ensure that the soft-livered end up embarrassed and regretful. To combat this, I planned to buy a mixer so that I could make my drinks weaker than Marcelle's. When you drink with these heavyweights, it's not so much a matter of matching them as it is a matter of keeping them company until they either drink themselves to sleep or come to the idea that they should leave before they pass out.

I spent a couple of minutes pretending to browse the shelves so that I didn't look like one of the drunks who, with mechanical urgency, swing the door open, walk decisively to the front of the line, place their crumpled cash in the metal pan, receive their chosen bottle, and bolt out the door after cracking the seal of the bottle and draining a shot. Two men came in and performed this exact ritual before I had gathered the nerve to approach the metal pan. The clerk eyed me a little differently than her other customers, as if she couldn't understand why such a timid young man would walk into this establishment alone, without some seedier friend to guide him through the process. I asked for the Wild Turkey, a brand that rarely left her shelf; the bottle was dusty, so she wiped it with a towel to restore its glow. She placed the bottle inside of a generic black plastic bag and slid it toward me.

Outside, the pack of beggars was nowhere to be found. I made it back to my building, where an NYPD Crime Scene Investigation van was still parked outside. A couple of detectives stood in hushed conversation with each other. Detective Larson was not around, but the two new cops looked me over as I got closer to the steps. They must have known that I lived in the building; they didn't stop me to ask any questions, and this was strangely comforting.

Back in the apartment I almost expected to see Randall pop his head out to watch me step through the door. For the first time, the place was all mine. I could stretch out in the living room if I wanted to. No one was going to steal my food out of the refrigerator. I had the urge to sweep all of the little action figures off the shelves and trash them, but that would have been evil.

I put the liquor in the kitchen and sat on the couch to regain myself. As horrific as the previous night had been, things were actually looking up for me. There was finally some silence in my life. I felt warm. Marcelle would arrive soon to tell me everything I needed to know about Contessa in order to pull her away from him. I had a whole apartment to myself. The towel was gone, and there were some jobs lined up for me that same week, so money was on the horizon. I was like a solitary mercenary who had lost contact with his unit and was forced to make his way back from behind enemy lines. The unattainable was within reach; it was only a matter of my remaining focused and unwavering. Marcelle would never be able to stop me from having Contessa for myself. She was my dream.

The bell rang. It was Marcelle. At last, my opportunity had arrived. I could see his blurred figure through the decorative glass of the front door like an unhatched creature fidgeting inside its membrane. The snow was falling more rapidly now. I composed myself one final time and opened the door. He rushed inside.

"Woo nigga, come on! It's cold as fuck outside. I need that drink ASAP." He snatched off his coat and hat and placed them on the hook.

"Yeah, I know. It looks crazy out there. Make yourself comfortable," I said reassuringly.

Once he took a seat on the couch, I moved to the kitchen to pour the drinks. Before I could remove the plastic seal, Marcelle was already at the kitchen threshold surveying the bottle. I hadn't heard his footsteps.

"What you know about that Wild Turkey, young man?" he called out, checking to see if I was pouring the right amount for him. I filled the glass halfway with no ice and gave it to him. He drank it all in one go.

"That's my get-in-the-door shot. Now let me get one for the couch, my nigga."

He took the drink back into the living room and sat on the couch. After a sip, he sat back and pulled out his phone. He looked comfortable. He was consumed in that small electronic realm of friends and strangers' lives that makes one feel so at peace. Part of me wanted to ignore him too and look at Contessa in my phone, but the plan had to be implemented. He was already becoming shut up within himself, showing so much unbounded energy yet unable to vocalize his intentions with clarity. His eyes went up and down with the scrolling screen in quick frantic jerks like a bird, and his thumb moved instinctively in intervals. I had to call out to him twice before he noticed I was sitting in the living room with him.

"Well, did you see the police van outside when you came in?" I almost shouted. I was already growing impatient.

He tossed the phone aside, but not too far away, with the screen still facing up.

"Yeah, I did. What happened? Somebody got shot?"

"My roommate did," I said flatly.

His eyes widened with excitement. "Where he got shot? On the sidewalk out there?"

"No, upstairs in his room." I sipped some of my own drink, waiting for the dread to show up on his face.

"Really?" His smile widened. "I want to see!"

"They won't let anyone inside the room. It's taped off," I said, disgusted with his cheerfulness, then reminded of the picture of Randall in my phone.

"Damn. That's crazy." He turned his head to look toward the stairwell leading up to the next floor. When he turned back toward me, a penetrating seriousness moved across his eyebrows. "You know this whole building is going to be haunted now. You gone have to move out, nigga."

His sudden coherence surprised me. "I was nice to Randall. I don't think his ghost will be angry with me. Why wouldn't it just go after the murderer?" I was proud of this response.

"Well, what did he do to get shot?"

"I'm not really sure. He kind of kept to himself."

"Either way, I'm trying to tell you. When somebody get murdered in a house, you gotta leave if you ain't trying to deal with they ghost. I saw it happen before. I didn't believe in it at first—you already know I'm covered with the blood of Jesus, nigga—but I can't even front. When my boy Tremaine got smoked? Man!" he cut himself short as if the memory was too horrifying to speak about.

He looked like he was telling the truth, but if I knew Marcelle it was most likely just a drug-induced hallucination. Letting him tell me about it might make him more relaxed. "I want to hear about it! Let me pour you another drink."

"This was back when I was in high school, back in California," he warmly began. "It was this house that was at the end of the block where the Mexican homie Sisito used to live. He was up in there with his momma, his dad, his grandma, and his older sister—she was fine as fuck, too. But Sisito, he was a little older than me, probably like nineteen or twenty, something like that, and he used to fuck with that angel dust. Well, one day he got real high and shot up his whole family—I shit you not, my nigga—then he shot hisself! He started shooting everybody at night, when everybody was sleep. The whole house was bloody."

He paused to reflect for a quick second.

"It was sad, though, because everybody walked past the house on they way to school every morning. His grandmother—everybody called her Ms. Gomez, and we didn't know if that was her real name or not, she would just smile and wave anyway, but she didn't really speak English like that. She was always wandering around in the front yard, you know, kind of looking lost, like she had that Alzheimer's, senile or whatever. Sometimes she would roam out the gate, but we looked out for her whenever she would wander outside in her bathrobe.

"Either way, after they all died, the house was boarded up, and me and some of my friends decided we should break in and look around, see if the blood was still there or maybe even some money. So we went up in there at night, like three or four of us, we had a flashlight and all that, and I swear, my nigga, we saw Ms. Gomez walking around in her bathrobe groaning and shit. And she had the bullet hole in the side of her head. We all saw it. I can call my nigga Monte *right now* if you don't believe me. He was there!"

"So what did you guys do when you saw her?" I asked, genuinely interested in the story now.

"What you think, we ran up out that motherfucker! I mean, it ain't like now; niggas didn't have no camera phone to record the shit. Plus, we was scared as fuck. Niggas ain't 'bout to be ghost hunting and shit for Discovery Channel," he shot back, snatching his drink back up to his lips. He spilled a little whiskey on his shirt. He was drunk now.

"I mean, it does sound crazy," I said, "but do you really think it was a ghost?"

"See, you too logical! I already know you on some 'that nigga Marcelle was probably just high' shit, but nah. This shit was for real. I hadn't even smoked no bud that day. Neither did none of my niggas. We was all sober. And we wasn't even expecting to see no shit like that. Everybody was too scared to go back the next day, but we told the story to some other people, and they decided to go in. We stood outside waiting to see what happened, but when they came out they said they didn't see nothing. I feel like they didn't see the ghost because they went in there during the day. We went in there at night, and that's when she liked to come out. Them niggas was scared to go in after dark. After that, though, I never questioned nobody that said they saw a ghost. That shit is real, my nigga!"

He was almost breathless.

"That's crazy, man. But it don't sound like Ms. Gomez wanted to mess with you. Maybe she was looking for Sisito?"

His eyes narrowed as he lowered the glass from his mouth. "Yeah, you could be right. But still, nigga. Shit ain't nothing to play with."

"Yeah. I feel you."

"Was he in the drug game?" Marcelle asked knowingly.

"I don't think so."

"What did he do?"

"Worked at a coffee shop some days, and he was one of those people who breaks your lock at the self-storage after you fall behind on the payments. Most of the stuff piled up around here is stuff he got to take home."

Marcelle looked over the apartment again, this time with genuine interest. "The nigga took them little action figures on the window sill? Was he twelve?"

"I don't know if he took those or if he bought them, but he liked having them around."

"Oh? So you was living in here with one of them hoarders?"

"I guess so."

"You ever got into it? He was one of them stealing-ass roommates?"

"No, not really. He ate some of my food every now and again, but that's just normal roommate stuff, you know?"

"I wish Jessica wouldn't touch any of my food!"

"You still stay with her?"

"Yeah, man." He took another drink. "I'm waiting for the perfect spot to open up so I can get out of there."

"I know Simone can't like that setup, right?"

"You already know she be tripping."

"Well, why don't you just move in with her? Wouldn't it be cheaper than getting your own place?" I took another sip, too, impressed with myself.

"I'm trying my best to put some space between us right now."

Marcelle presented his glass for a refill, and I obliged him immediately, aware that my opening in the conversation had arrived naturally. I'd feigned interest in his ghost story so intently that I hadn't noticed how full my glass was. He was excited but a little slothful. His face brightened when I brought the glass of whiskey back to him.

"Why do you say they're crazy, though? Don't they all act right if you're having good sex?" I paused. "I mean, Simone seemed really cool." I was anxious to hear his response.

"Man, she just got issues, you know? Like her dad is in the pen for some kind of bank robbery situation. I think he might have killed somebody when everybody else was trying to get away, or maybe he was the one that got shot and that's why he got caught. Something crazy like that. So, you know, she got issues over that, like she don't need a man but she really want one bad, you know? People trip like that, pretending like they can live without the one thing they really need. But she smart, too. Like she had to make up for her daddy's dumbass ways. She never even went to college. She just pay the cheapest rent possible and draw all day. She might get famous off that shit one day. Her shit kind of tight, but she don't really give a fuck about showing her work to nobody. I'm like, 'Simone? When you gone put this shit up in a gallery or something? You always want to go to the museum and look at the next artist work, but your shit is way better!'"

"And what does she say to *that*?" I asked feverishly.

"'My work isn't made for everyone. People who like it will gravitate to it naturally.' You know, shit like that."

I was beginning to feel angry. I didn't like the way he spoke about Contessa and her background so dismissively. She was an artist forged out of misery, and all he could do was think about putting her and her work on the auction block. He mishandled practically every topic relating to her. He'd been crass at the museum, and he was being an outright clown now. The longstanding question remained: What did she like about Marcelle?

It was true that Marcelle was what many people would call handsome, and he did have a freewheeling, humorous personality, but was that enough for someone like Contessa? She had to have higher standards, had to be attracted to something deeper that couldn't be picked up on over drinks at a bar. I'd known Marcelle for years, and he never seemed to have a thought that wasn't concerned with "getting money" or "fucking bitches." The little schemes he came up with to achieve those ends might've had some trace of intellect or cleverness, but there wasn't anything profound about him. Now, I hadn't seen him for a few years, and in that time he might have developed some depth, but that hadn't seemed to be the case at the party, or at the museum, or even now in my apartment, and I didn't think he had any reason to hide that part of his personality. None of it made sense. The same woman who spoke so elegantly about art while carrying herself with so much dignity was dating a buffoon, a drug dealer, a womanizer, and a drunk.

"It still doesn't add up," I went on. "She seems like a really special woman. Why would you be trying to get away from her?"

He turned his wavering, drunken head toward me, grinned, and said, "Addy, you always been a little simp when it came to the bitches. A nigga ain't trying to be tied to just one for too long. Too many out there to be stuck on one."

"But what if she's a good one, Marcelle?" I was hoping that the seriousness in my voice wouldn't shake him from his nonchalant mood.

"Then she can be one of my good ones. A nigga want a basket of good ones."

"The good ones don't want to be in anyone's *basket*."

"And that's what's wrong with these hoes." He took his phone out of his pocket. "Look at this," he said as he opened a photo album and began swiping through a collection of naked women. In one of the pictures, there were two women kissing and cupping each other's breasts. At the bottom of the picture were Marcelle's two feet covered by dirty socks, showing that he'd taken the picture lying on his back as the two women stood before him. "See! That's how I'm trying to have it. Every day. I met them two in Vegas a year ago. Ranika and Kelis!" He was very proud of himself, waving the picture in my face.

"Did they know each other already?"

"Yeah, they was together."

"Is Simone into that kind of thing, too?"

"No, and that's part of the problem."

I was silently relieved, but took great pains not to show it on my face. "What does she say when you bring it up to her?"

"I'm not the one," he said mockingly, his voice tuned up an octave.

At that moment, I began wondering what would be the best way to murder Marcelle. His presence had suddenly become intolerable. I wanted to rid the world—Contessa's world—of his indecency, his lack of reverence. He was a bubbling, spreading stain coming closer and closer to engulfing the last bit of beauty that existed in this world. A kind of amoeba, he was able to shift shape and direction simultaneously in his greedy effort to devour. Impure. Deceitful. A character worthy of assassination.

I was almost willing to accept whatever consequences might come from such an act. Prison. Revenge. Shame. None of those mattered. But the thought of murder arose so suddenly that I almost forgot to consider the single most important factor: How would Contessa feel? She might find out the truth and come to despise me forever, especially if she really held strong feelings for Marcelle. What were the contents of those secret, isolated moments they shared? How did she really feel whenever he walked through her door or met up with her for a date? Did he bore her? What if she was waiting for me? These unanswered questions were all that stayed my hand and kept me from snapping Marcelle's neck.

"Where does Simone even live, anyway?" I cut in desperately. He was drunk and swiping through his phone. An intermediate moment passed between his hearing my question and finally having it register well enough to pull his attention away from the screen.

My meditation on murder flickered about again, only to evaporate once his feeble expression locked onto me. One of the sweetest pleasures of the human imagination is the secret right we all have to imagine annihilating another person even while looking at him. Far from being limited to conflicts between friends, I'm sure that lovers partake in this kind of daydream so often that it becomes a ritual, especially between the most faithful couples. How else could one purge that accumulation of slights and offenses which, when taken individually, not only amount to unacknowledged annoyances, but a collection amassed over months and then years? It renders a homicidal urge so justified, yet forbidden, that the slighted finally settles for the silent, transparent, and evanescent killing that takes place behind the eyelids.

"What you say?" he asked.

"Does Simone live in Bed-Stuy?" I rephrased the question.

"Oh, yeah. She stay right around the block from you. You know that new building on Marion? She up in that motherfucker," he huffed with a degree of prestige.

Sensing that subtle gloat, I took the opportunity to play it up a bit. "You been in there before, then?"

"Nigga what? All up and through that bitch. Shit is tight!"

"What's so tight about it?"

"Man, it's like 95 percent white, and they not them dirty-ass hipster white people—these is white boys with bread. Like they probably in tech or something. Half of them is blond, too. You rarely see a real blond-beast-looking-ass white boy. They not trying to be all close to niggas. But with them in there, you know that shit is decked out. Floor-to-ceiling windows, a gym, washer and dryer in every unit, shit like that."

"So how does she afford it?"

"She got into one of them low-income units, it's like three of them in there. She had to apply on some artist-type shit. She got it, though, on some fuck shit!"

It was true—I had never heard of anyone who managed to win one of those stupid housing lotteries for low-income apartments in otherwise ritzy buildings. I always thought they were a scam. Contessa got one. I silently congratulated her and embraced this new bit of evidence proving her chosenness. No one but Contessa was worthy of such a prize. Regal accommodations for an unsung queen. A building with an elevator. Every conceivable comfort needed to be in place for beauty like hers. Amenhotep III is known to have had an entire lake, one mile long and a quarter of a mile wide, carved out of the Egyptian landscape in honor of his wife, Tiye. There was no way Marcelle felt the same. The idea of extending himself in the name of someone else, someone sacred, whose existence was an ideal more than an attainable thing—the act of giving himself over completely to both the person and what she represented—was a foreign concept to him.

But I would be unfair to lay such an indictment at his feet alone. This sense of longing to genuinely appreciate someone didn't seem important to most people I met, and it was frightening and isolating to walk around and visit people and watch movies with them and never feel anything special. To hold hands and shrivel up inside because of how boring it all was. It often felt that way to me until Contessa appeared. My relationships were more like consensual opportunities to practice sex. We trusted each other and found one another attractive but not interesting. I went on dates with women whose names I couldn't remember until I had a chance to look at their text messages. There were times when I was happy when the woman offered to pay, otherwise I wasn't going to eat a full meal. I even got so far as to meet the parents of one girlfriend. Sarah and I had been together long enough that it seemed appropriate. The four of us sat at the dinner table without speaking. Sarah and I usually did the same thing when it was only the two of us.

"Pour me another shot, my nigga," he mumbled, pretending to be dejected.

I almost felt sorry for him. My little strategy had worked perfectly. There really was no further need for him; he had practically become another Randall to me. Out of deference to courtesy and tradition, or, I guess, for old times' sake, I didn't move to kick him out. I went to the kitchen and poured him another drink. I even poured another for myself.

"Man, I got to figure out what I'm gone do," he said as I came back with the next round of drinks.

"About what?"

"I need to find another spot."

"What's wrong with Jessica's?"

"Aside from sleeping on the couch? You know Simone be tripping about me staying with another broad, even though I was already living with Amanda when I met her."

"Have you started looking?"

"Yeah, but I ain't found nothing that I want to pay for. It's a one-bedroom in East New York, not too far from here."

"How much do they want?"

"Nineteen."

"Damn."

"Exactly."

"I would offer you the room upstairs," I said toyingly, "but you know ..."

"I'm all the way cool on that haunted room shit."

And so another thought struck me. I might only have to sit back and let the market finish Marcelle off for me. With every rise in rent prices, a new wave of residents was pushed out of Bed-Stuy, farther east into Brownsville and East New York. Although Randall's room was a murder scene, once it was cleaned no one would be the wiser. I wished I could rent it out and keep the apartment. Contessa—magical, sweet Contessa—had chanced upon a low-income apartment, so she wasn't going anywhere soon. But poor, unlucky Marcelle, with his floundering drug business, was being rendered obsolete. It was all but impossible to sell his goods on the street because of the cameras and the police and his outsider status in the Brooklyn drug market. And with no traditional work history for years, no beneficial ties to his family back in California as a guarantor, there was no way for him to secure a lease. Even the last-ditch effort of couch surfing was out of his reach because no one beside Jessica would have the patience to put up with a womanizing drug dealer. His only option, then, if he wanted to stay in Brooklyn at all, was to move east, which meant tumbling down the totem pole of relevance. He'd be marked as poor. His days would consist of poorly stocked corner stores, infrequent trains, police surveillance towers, and very few visits from friends. With Uber, he could still maintain ties to the people he knew here, show up to their parties from time to time, but the cab fees would discourage him, and soon he would be stuck in his dim apartment with his drugs and his mice.

Now he was back in his phone searching for pictures of the apartment in East New York. "Look at that," he said stretching to hand me the phone.

There were four pictures of a shabby, empty studio apartment, taken at night so the windows framed a ghostly darkness whose contrast with the eggshell white paint of the walls spelled dread and misery. The bathroom was cramped; if he sat on the toilet, his knees would have to touch the bathtub.

"It's not all that, but it'll be all mine. Not that far from the train either."

"I feel you," I said, stretching to hand the phone back to him.

"I'm going to see the landlord tomorrow and see what he talking about."

We sat silently, thumbing through our phones.

A few minutes later, Marcelle looked up and said, "Oh shit, I forgot! You need some bud?"

I declined. It was quiet again.

We sat that way for a long time. Silent. Unmoving. It was comforting to be shut out from someone, sitting with your fellow human without the burden of acknowledgement. When you sit quietly on a train packed with other passengers, you're filled with expectation. You want to arrive at your destination. You don't want any of those silent, smelly people to bother you. It's a hostile situation. You avoid eye contact. This is how I felt for a long time whenever I walked outside or found myself around other people. My life had become a long train ride, only there was no destination until I saw Contessa.

For a moment, I forgot about Marcelle entirely and searched for information about Contessa's new building. The apartment buildings, erected on a plot of land where three older homes once stood, was named "139 Hull Street." Composed of thirty-two units, the apartments ranged from three-thousand-a-month studios to sixty-two-hundred-a-month three-bedrooms complete with terraces or faux balconies. Except for the studios, each apartment came with a washer and dryer. Every one had stainless steel refrigerators with French doors, Brazilian cherrywood floors, and corner stand-alone showers complemented by jacuzzi tubs. One noteworthy feature was the building's wireless charging system, achieved by miles of transmitter coil embedded behind walls and beneath countertops. There were deck chairs, a small swimming pool, and barbecue grills (also stainless steel) on the rooftop. Contessa was really living in the lap of luxury. What kind of food was she eating? A sparse, vegan diet? Maybe. But I chose to believe that Contessa wasn't obsessed with quinoa.

The gulf between Marcelle and I widened. I had no further use for him.

"I think I'm going to try and lay it down, bro. I'm drunk," I said, still looking at the pictures in my phone.

"I feel you, my nigga. I'm faded, too. Let me make moves before it start coming down too hard outside."

We rose from our seats and shook hands. Before he walked to the door, he asked for one final drink. I poured the whiskey triumphantly and looked on with pity as he finished it. He turned to walk out. I slammed

and locked the door before he had even made it to the
sidewalk.

LET ME LOOK AT YOU　　155

and locked the door before he had even made it to the
sidewalk.

Chapter Ten

AS I MENTIONED EARLIER, MY RELATIONSHIP WITH MY FAMILY BACK IN VIRGINIA WASN'T THE strongest. With the departure of my sister for the federal penitentiary, I lost all motivation to visit any of those people from my past. So it's understandable that, during the holiday season, I am at my loneliest. No gatherings, no outings or road trips, no special recipes or aromas in my kitchen. I associate all of those trivialities with my awful family and the wretched state of Virginia. But I can't wallow in depression or regret for very long, and it was just my luck that, before Thanksgiving that year, Contessa took a trip home. Her absence had two benefits. First, it gave me time to think of the next strategy; now that I knew where she lived, I had to plot out my approach. There was also plenty of free time, which I filled by binge-watching *Turncoat*, a new show about a double-crossing spy.

Even in my childhood, I don't remember ever being too excited about television. Sure, I enjoyed watching cartoons and action movies, but the stunts and antics never seemed achievable for me, so I was always able to keep the TV at arm's distance. The fun that people had on TV shows was too fun, the money they won on game shows was too much money—at least compared to what I experienced in my own life. My friends would act out different fighting moves they saw in the movies, and I'd play along even though I knew I would never be a ninja or a wrestler. I don't think my friends were that hopeless. Even if they didn't become ninjas, they held onto the spirit of the TV prototype throughout life and used it as motivation. I think this is the secret of television, to let those characters come and live inside us and guide us when an appropriate situation arises.

With the holiday season near its end, New Year's Eve arrived, and Contessa returned to New York for the festivities. Naturally, with her reappearance, the spell cast on me by *Turncoat* was lifted, and I saw the show for what it was: a distraction at best, and a socially accepted form of dissociation disguised as escapism at the very worst.

I found out about Contessa's return after checking her profile page. She came back to Brooklyn in high spirits; there were new pictures of her with her family members, including her precious old grandmother. I was doubly satisfied to see that she had taken no pictures with her father, so it was that much easier to believe Marcelle's story about him. There were also no pictures of Marcelle. She didn't love him, and what's more she couldn't possibly show up back home with a drug dealer from New York. The matter was settled. They weren't married, Marcelle talked about her like she was dirt, she hadn't posted any pictures of him on her profile for the holidays. Their relationship meant nothing. She was waiting for me. There was no more time to plot. The New Year was upon us, and Contessa deserved real happiness. I couldn't bear the thought of staying away from her any longer. At that very moment, staring at my clock as it read "12:31 a.m." on New Year's Day, I vowed that the next time I saw Contessa, she would know everything.

Chapter Eleven

I STOOD ACROSS THE STREET FROM HER BUILDING. IT WAS MODEST FROM MY standpoint, and only after watching its entrance for two hours did I see that most of the tenants were rich and white. Another hour later, with no sign of her, I left.

The next day, a Tuesday, the snow stopped, and my little miracle came outside. She wore a long purple coat as she walked toward Rockaway Avenue. As soon as she turned the corner, I started following her. I tracked her down into the train station, where I pulled back some so that she wouldn't see me. When the train arrived, I boarded the same car as her, taking care to keep a few bodies between us to obscure her view of me. She stood holding the rail with a sad and slightly annoyed look on her face. Our train left Brooklyn and eventually got rid of us at Fourteenth Street. She took the stairs.

Outside, she crossed the street and rushed inside the computer store. A few minutes later, I went inside, too.

I was on the brink of panic because there was no sign of her, only the shifting shoulders and darting bodies of customers, similar to the subway, similar to the supermarket, similar even to the museum exhibit. People shuffled between tables, held expensive phones in their hands, and assessed the sound quality of the other devices. I saw a metallic green phone, much better than the one I owned, and I wanted so badly to touch it, but I had to find Contessa first.

"I have to have the green one!" said a child. His mother flagged down one of the employees, who materialized beside them with a smile.

The employee's self-assured expression worried me. He looked like someone who could disarm me, make me feel unworthy of that new green phone and in turn compel me to try and prove to him that I deserved it. Each and every device in that store would be better off with me, if only the tech people would be reasonable.

I looked over again and saw the employee tearing the plastic wrapper away from the small rectangular box. Very carefully, so as not to bend or dent the cardboard, he removed the lid and revealed a much shinier metallic green phone than the one that was on display. He handed the phone to the little boy, whose grin was far more sinister than the clerk's. The mother smiled, too.

"Hey, Adrian. What are you up to? Are you getting the ten?"

I looked to the left and saw her. I could not lose this precious moment again. "Actually, I came in here to see you." I paused and savored the silence.

"What do you mean?"

"I was across the street and saw you walk in here, so I figured I'd come and say hello."

"That's nice! Since you're here, can you help me with something?"

"Sure."

She took my arm and led me up the stairs to where the drones were sold.

We reached the third floor, and I followed Contessa to one of the stations where the new Zzo cams were on display. For $350.00 and decent credit, you could purchase one of the flying cameras and have your own personal paparazzi film you and snap your picture from practically any angle. A considerable improvement on the selfie stick, the Zzo was hands-free, about the size of a large marble or jawbreaker candy, with two thin propellers that straddled the surface of this small sphere when it wasn't in flight. You controlled the Zzo with your phone, making it hover a few feet away from you to record. Various sensors in the little orb kept it from crashing into other objects, and its lightness made it relatively harmless to human skin. It was one of the best drone cameras on the market, featuring a ten-element lens, facial recognition, thirteen megapixels, HiLite flash, night vision, 5x zoom, 2160p (4K) HD video recording, a motion sensor, a rechargeable lithium ion battery allowing for twenty-four hours of continuous, simultaneous flight-and-record time, and it came in five assorted colors. Contessa studied the silver one.

There seemed to be no backdrop that failed to accentuate her profile. At the party, beneath the red lights and shrouded in smoke, she took on a bluesy, almost dangerous luster that combined with her toying and seductive movement on the dance floor; at the museum she was knowing but distant; here in the store, she took up a sophisticated stance amid all the technology and pristine video advertisements. Her slender hands looked elegant holding the little orb, two fingers pinching and rotating it delicately as though she might put it in her mouth like a small chocolate and crush it with her pretty teeth.

I stepped closer, so that I was now standing beside her, and her scent, akin to a thick maple syrup, met my nose.

"That one looks nice," I said, looking down at her hands.

My compliment pleased her, and for the first time in a very long time, I saw her smile.

"Are you going to buy that one?" I asked.

"I think this is the one."

As she turned to look for a store clerk, one of them appeared between us. The man's sudden presence irked me. I wanted to grab him by his collar and snatch him away, but Contessa looked delighted; at least he wasn't Marcelle.

"Do you folks need help with anything?" His name tag read "Scott." Scott stood at about five-foot-nine— the same height as me—and although he had on the same uniform as the other employees (light blue polo shirt, khaki pants, white sneakers), his paleness set him apart. He wore glasses, and his brown hair was much longer on the top of his head than on the sides. His slenderness made his bones sharp. His Adam's apple protruded like a triangle beneath the skin of his neck. He looked smart, and this made me feel reassured. Whoever hired Scott had made a good decision. It was difficult to be engaged by this frail, innocent salesman and not feel intoxicated with the urge to buy. Purchasing a new phone or drone with his assistance was going to feel like an honor for us.

This characteristic—polite tenderness and warmth—was the common feature of all the salespeople in the store. The company had taken its hiring practices very seriously, and one saw how its diverse staff was united by an overarching principle: "Kill them with kindness." Normally, a store hires its staff from the surrounding community, which makes the customer feel like she is shopping in the local market of her village, as though the products for sale do not have their origins in distant countries; the items could have been brought to the market on a loaded cart pulled by horses. It makes us feel at home. But this is not the point of the computer store; instead it seeks to let us know that the purchase of one of its devices is the first step in gaining access to the entire planet, whether by reading encyclopedias in different languages on a phone or watching a soccer match in Central Asia on a tablet. So it follows that the staff in each store is a microcosm of the world that awaits you. Scott was white, but his whiteness took on a new significance when placed in the setting of the tech store. He looked like a world citizen, not an American. Aside from Scott, the other clerks seemed to have been partially hired for their multicultural appeal: one clerk wore a hijab, another two were Southeast Asian and black, one used a wheelchair, and another was a trans woman. Every single human was invited; each and every one of us could find solace—if only temporarily—so long as we took interest in the devices.

"That's definitely the best personal drone on the market," Scott said, "and I'm not just telling you that because I work here. I'm completely addicted to mine." He showed us the drone in his pocket and smiled warmly.

Along with singlehandedly luring the mass of humankind into the next generation of telecommunication, what other ambitions did these smiling, affable, and concerned henchmen have for me? It made perfect sense to be as winsome as possible if your goal was to put a device in everyone's hand. My solitary suspicion about the intentions of the benevolent tech store clerk made little sense. Did Contessa ask herself similar questions?

"Can I transfer the pictures from this old twelve onto the Zzo without using the cloud?"

"I can do that for you here in the store!" Scott assured her.

Contessa turned to me. "Okay, Addy, which color do you like more, the silver one or the blue one?"

"The blue one."

"Me, too!" She handed the blue Zzo to Scott, who turned and led us to the cash registers. As we approached the front of the line, I could feel some of the crowd beginning to pay closer attention; we looked special as the next clerk rang us up at the counter. These cameras were expensive. Out of modesty I stepped away from Contessa when the cashier, a short Japanese girl with braces and the quick, panicked movements of a squirrel, asked Contessa to slide her credit card.

With the transaction complete, I rejoined Contessa, and we walked outside. "We have to find somewhere to sit down. It's so cold out here," I thought. I wanted to take hold of her.

"Are you hungry?" I asked instead.

"Yes! Let's eat, and you can show me how to set this up."

The mental picture of Marcelle that had been hovering in the back of my mind all day evaporated. I took Contessa by her arm and led her into a nearby diner.

"Let's sit here," I said as we made it inside the Crimson Diner.

"Perfect."

We picked up the menus. Contessa said she only wanted French fries, so I ordered two orders to share. The waitress left, and Contessa presented the drone box on the table. She used her thumbnail to slice the thin tape placed around the box in different places, then slid a cardboard tray out. The drone was nestled securely inside; it took her a couple of tries to pop it out. When she finally did, the little device rolled out onto the table. I stopped it before it fell to the floor.

"That was almost the end of that!" I said.

"Right?" she laughed. She handed me the instructions.

"Do you have your phone?" I asked. "It says you have to sync them."

She handed me her phone.

"You have to put in your password."

"Three-six-seven-three," she said.

The setup was pretty simple; we only needed to download the appropriate app. From there, Contessa could control the drone with her phone. I returned her phone to her, and she managed to operate the drone's camera. She snapped a picture of us seated at the table from above. An old man seated across from us noticed the camera's flash. He shook his head at us with great disgust, maybe even heartbreak, and slinked out of his booth. With shameless disapproval, he muttered and looked back at us as he placed his hat on his head and left the restaurant.

"We're going to make so many people mad!" Contessa said as she turned off the drone and put it back in the box. "What's your phone number? I'm going to send my first video to you."

I recited my number immediately.

The waitress returned and placed two small baskets of French fries between us. Contessa asked if I wanted ketchup. I nodded, and she poured a small dollop into the corner of my basket, then did the same thing for her own. We ate silently, looking outside at the immense indifference and focus of the people going past. Each person walked busily without regard for those in front of or behind him, but this pedestrian solitude, this commute in isolation, was maintained by sharp, lucid, almost tactical concentration. Every citizen applied enormous effort to forget about the scatter and commotion about him, to reach his elusive destination before its inevitable disappearance. How had I chanced upon Contessa in this disarray, this overabundance of shoulders and hats and layers swimming around and dodging one another in the street? It couldn't have happened any other way.

"Isn't it wild how many people there are?" she asked, still staring.

"It is."

"The crazy thing is, there's so many other cities in the world with a lot more people. I read once that Tokyo has twice as many people as New York. And India has ten cities bigger than New York."

"But none of them are quite like here."

"You're right." She looked back at the fries. "You have to be a special level of demented to force yourself to be here. Look at everybody. They all look miserable. Everybody looks lonely."

"Yeah, I can see that."

"It's true. No matter how many people you meet in this city, you still end up lonely. Not the way you feel in an empty room, but the way you feel if you go to a big concert by yourself."

"That would definitely make me feel lonely."

"You'd think it would be easy to connect with other people. I don't know. Maybe it is for some people, but I think this city forces you to be lonely. If people could really connect with someone, they'd wake up and leave here forever."

"But where would they go?"

"Where would you go?" She turned and faced me.

"I don't know. Back home to Virginia, I guess."

"I could never go back home to live. I don't even like to visit."

She always looked so happy in her profile pictures from South Carolina. "What's wrong with your home?"

"I don't really have family back there now. My dad is in prison. My mom is stuck on Jesus and thinks I'm living in sin because I take pictures."

"What kinds of pictures?"

"Regular pictures. Of people. I haven't taken any nudes yet, but I will soon."

"Don't you have any friends back home?"

"I had a best friend, but she died in a car accident three years ago."

"I'm sorry."

"It's okay. At first, it was terrible. I couldn't sleep. But now I'm starting to think about it less."

"Was she driving?"

"No, her boyfriend was. He was drunk."

"Damn."

"I was in the backseat. I'm the only one who made it."

"Wow, Simone. I had no idea—"

"I know. I haven't really said a lot about it, but for some reason I feel comfortable sharing with you."

"Simone, you can talk to me about anything."

She smiled at me and ate more fries. Suddenly, as though I had been blind to it before, I noticed her complete and utter sadness, which had always been locked in place across her face. I had overlooked this feature of hers in the past, but now it stood out like the distant mountaintop towers of a castle against the moonlit sky. "These artist-types," I thought to myself. "They're always so unbelievably sad."

At last, the fries were finished. Contessa looked at her phone and began gathering her things. "I have to go uptown now. I'm a little late," she said, smiling and pulling her things closer to herself. "Don't worry, though, I'll text you later tonight."

We stood up and hugged for longer than we ever had before. This meant that things had changed between us. We were close now. I watched her disappear into the throng outside.

That night when I made it home, I noticed a change. Something new was growing inside me. This rejuvenation was a sweet spread of health and good cheer; my general mood blossomed. I could suddenly breathe more deeply. I say with no reservations that I was completely happy. It was while in the midst of this all-encompassing ecstasy that I received my first message from Contessa.

> Sorry for being so depressing earlier.

That's ok. I like hearing about your life! I sent back.

After a ten-minute delay, which felt like an eternity and nearly shattered my newfound confidence in Contessa's interest in me, she sent me a curious text: the number 9119 and then a link. I opened it and was prompted to enter a passcode. A menu appeared on my phone and showed that I was her only "viewer." Contessa had uploaded a video with the Zzo just a few minutes earlier. Satisfied that she had actually spent the gap thinking about and preparing something for me, I clicked the link.

It was a ten-second clip that began with an empty portion of a desk. At about the two-second mark, Contessa's hand slid into view, pushing her New York State ID into the frame. Her hand disappeared, and all of the information on her ID appeared in clear focus. Her hand returned, flipped the card over, and left the frame again. The back of the card was visible for a few more seconds before the scene cut to black. There was no caption no words, only the hand, the card, and the information it contained, including the dated photo of Contessa on the ID. She wore a ponytail and a smile. She looked twenty-one. The background was a dull bureaucratic blue, the smile at once contrived and authentic; she had been compelled to smile in order to defeat the dreaded backdrop and stop its misery-inducing tone from drowning out her beauty completely, but she also couldn't help smiling because her day at the DMV was at its end. So this was Contessa's face under the influence of two competing moods: farce and relief.

I took note of the information to the right of the picture; her name, her address (139 Hull Street, Apt 1C, Brooklyn NY 11233), her date of birth (November 13, 1988), the date the card was issued (May 12, 2021), and the date that it would expire (November 13, 2025). Her ID number spanned the top of the card (R9335126), and her physical attributes were listed along the bottom of the card (Sex: F, Hair: Black, Weight: 125 lbs.). The back of the card featured her signature, along with various numbers whose purpose evaded me, though I was certain they would reveal even more information about her if only I knew how and where to use them.

The video of the ID card was absolutely the clearest, sharpest image of anything I'd ever seen on a screen. It gave me the feeling I might be able to pick up the card and put it in my own pocket.

Though her short clip confused me, I nevertheless secretly welcomed this glimpse into her private world. I suppose I took it as some kind of joke, honestly. I had no interest in defrauding Contessa; I only wanted to possess her. Strangely, seeing her address and information on the screen comforted me like nothing had ever before. I might say that I felt closer to her than I ever had on the dance floor.

Immediately after sending the first clip, another showed up beneath it. This next video was exactly like the one before it, only now she slid her social security card into view: Simone Sharita Nelson, 249-35-9315. This made me frown. Was it her actual Social Security card? Was this some sort of joke?

Why did you send me all that? I finally typed back.

Because I want you to see ME. She sent another link labeled "live feed." I clicked it, and her bedroom appeared, dimly lit, but I could make out the bed with its sheets pulled back.

At that moment, I threw off calling her "Contessa" once and for all and settled on her real name: Simone Sharita Nelson, which had an official ring to it and came coupled with an element of honor. After so much time spent waiting in the shadows, I was finally being openly invited into her world. Quite frankly, all of this was beginning to feel surreal. My inherent and longstanding inability to give myself over to anything or anyone was finally about to crumble completely. Did I dare hesitate? Of course not, not after all the waiting and plotting and thinking; not after besting Marcelle and even sleeping in the realm of the dead with Randall's bloody clothes languishing in the room upstairs. I became ecstatic with an insatiable hunger for Simone and her content. Her pictures, her footage, in a word: *Her*.

On the screen, she appeared like an apparition in the dim light. She crawled into her bed naked and lowered the lights a little more. The Zzo registered the scene perfectly despite the low light. After just a few minutes, I could tell that she was fast asleep. I turned out my own light and let this image of Simone illuminate my room. We went to sleep together.

And this became the nature of our relationship; I rarely ever saw Simone in person again. This daily, nonstop feed of information satisfied me and never once interfered with my own routine.

As you might imagine, her content went far beyond selfies or short clips of her riding roller coasters or walking through Manhattan with her friends, the kind of content that tells lies openly. Each selfie is an imposter and a fraud, because we rarely feel as confident as we try to portray ourselves. Any image that denies the heartbreak and confusion of the person we see reveals nothing to us.

My relationship with Simone was one of pure revelation.

Some days I would open the link to watch Simone, and she'd be sitting in her room alone, looking into her phone. She'd be in bed, swiping, smiling, laughing at a video or else typing madly as she responded to text messages. In those moments, I knew it was Marcelle who was on the other end, sometimes annoying her, sometimes seducing her. Before very long it seemed she had forgotten about me, but this did not worry me; in fact, it comforted me to know that she never shut me out, that she included me so intimately in her daily life. I was a kind of silent, nonjudging guardian or watchful eye, and though we never spoke about it, I knew that I was a comfort to her.

And so it was a rain-soaked evening in April when I watched her leave the room and return holding Marcelle by the hand. She led him to the bed. He had grown his hair out a bit and lost a little weight, a result of the struggles of winter. She kissed him on the forehead. I leaned in to watch more carefully.

I felt serene. I had spent so much time plotting and wringing my hands and hoping for some sort of acceptance from Simone. Now I had more than anyone else ever had. I used to hate my phone and my laptop in many ways, but when they became the tools I needed to access Simone so immediately, so transparently, I had to concede that I had finally come to love them. Amid the trillions of connections, pages, videos, comments, profiles, movies, and emails, this vast desert of the Internet offered me one oasis, and she was Simone. I would never stop watching her. She had become an extension of me. We were at last tethered together in the deep space of the web. I have to say once and for all that I was happy. While others argued incessantly about the merits of various TV shows or looked up "swollen bump in armpit" or responded breathlessly to think pieces about politics or racism, I live-streamed Simone day and night.

Maybe it was some cosmic test of my resolve, or simply fate, but after a month of watching Simone go about her day-to-day activities, something different happened. Up to that point, Marcelle would visit Simone two or three times a week. He came at night and left in the morning. I didn't see much of him because most of their time together took place in the dark. I didn't mind either way. Then one day he walked into Simone's room carrying a blue Nike duffle bag. Far from jealousy, I felt a rush of satisfaction.

It was like watching a movie. Two days after he moved in, Marcelle's first guest visited while Simone was away. They polluted the room for twenty minutes with a shared blunt. Then they left together. Three days later, not twenty minutes after Simone had left for work, a different friend arrived. Instead of the bed, they made use of the desk chair. In the space of two weeks, five different women kept him company. He sustained this regimen for four months.

It was a Wednesday afternoon when Simone returned home early from work and caught Marcelle in bed with Brianna. Simone explained that she had a feeling about what he was up to but was too afraid to check the footage from the camera in the corner of the room.

"That's a camera?" Marcelle asked.

Simone told them they may as well finish, since they'd had an audience all this time. Brianna apologized and started to dress herself. Marcelle apologized and explained the difference between "feelings" and "sex." Simone nodded. Her poise frightened Marcelle, and he began to dress as well. He reached out to put his hand on Simone's shoulder, but she didn't give him any reaction. She said Brianna and Marcelle didn't have to leave, that she wasn't not tired and didn't need the bed right now. They were confused and afraid. Simone remained calm. Marcelle tried to grab her hand, and Simone, in response, slapped him across the mouth. She then wrapped her hands around his throat and squeezed. Brianna screamed. Simone's swiftness caused Marcelle to lose his balance. He tumbled backward with Simone's hands still around his throat. The video quality was such that I could see the bloody scars forming as Simone's nails plunged deeper into

Marcelle's flesh. Suddenly, she released him, and Marcelle recovered himself. "I deserved that," he said, and Simone agreed as she peeled small shards of skin from beneath her fingernails. He finished dressing. Brianna scrambled out of the apartment. He grabbed a few things from a drawer, stuffed them into his duffel, and said, "I'm gone." Simone sat alone for a long time. Then she slipped into bed and fell fast asleep.

After that, her video feed went blank. I didn't see her for a long time. I understood why she wouldn't want to be on display, but it still felt like I had been shut out. What could I do but wait? So I waited. I waited four months before her feed went live again. All she did was slide a handwritten note into view: "You're invited. Pruitt Gallery. Friday. 11/5. 6PM."

This time, when I entered the gallery, I noticed right away how much smaller it was. Simone wasn't as big-time as Mdembe yet, but that made the visit better. I didn't have to wait long to get inside either. A woman with blond locs stood behind the counter. Her earlobes sagged under the weight of wooden earrings, and she wore an entire system of necklaces and what looked like dagger-shaped rings on her fingers. With her black lipstick, she gave me a cold look; or, rather, she wore a stony expression until sight of me prompted a change. Then she smiled. She was gorgeous. Her forehead and face were spotless and smooth, but her eyes, surrounded by shadow, told the rest of the story. She was tired or weary or both, and when she had finished directing me to the exhibit, I looked back and saw that she had fallen back into the same grim repose as before.

I walked down a long hallway with doors leading to different exhibits. They were all curious and quite forward-thinking, if the titles beside the entrances were anything to go by. They read like dissertation titles. They pointed to numerous and sophisticated concepts, far beyond my understanding. They made ordinary words into mysteries. Beside one entrance, for example, a card read, *Bizarre Blackness—Refractive Silence and Dark Symbiosis in the Black Body*. Another sign read, *We Got You: Aquatic Remembrance of Eco-Racist Trauma*. A third placard simply read *Fuck America*. Many people were gathered around this last one, and everyone who walked out looked self-assured and satisfied. One woman announced as she returned to the hallway, "Oh, this one is *lit* lit!" and her girlfriend replied, "Bitch!" Someone else, I couldn't see who, yelled out, "Hell yeah, nigga! Fuck America!" People laughed and clapped. Music erupted, and they started dancing.

At the end of the hall was Simone's exhibit. The title was *What Do U C?* Inside, the walls were covered entirely with photos. They were portraits, but the stares of the faces—the drifting, lolling monotony of the eyes—somehow fell below the prestige of a portrait. No one in any of the pictures was posing. Everyone had blank expressions. Their features were subdued but not quite serene. They were searching for something without being curious. People look more interested when they're searching for a matching pair of socks in a drawer.

There must have been over a thousand faces, each subject in a different state of dress. Some wore work clothes, some pajamas, and a few wore nothing at all. They had different backgrounds, of course. The viewer got a good sense of all the little things people do to decorate and change the appearance of their dreary rooms. Most had white walls, or a kind of light gray bone color covered with pictures or interrupted by plants. Some of the subjects had guests over, and their guests were also looking into the camera. Everyone was looking at Simone. And over in the corner, five images to the right, about a foot above the floor, I saw the picture of me—one I'd never posed for and did not know how she'd taken—wearing the same blank expression as all the others. I looked tired; whatever excitement I felt for Simone hid behind my dreary eyes.

As I walked over for a better look, a small group walked into the room. They stopped in front of some pictures on the opposite wall. They pointed to themselves and took turns posing for pictures next to their pictures. Another group jostled in and did the same thing in front of their pictures. They held their phones up high. The phones guided them. They could not see but for the cameras in their phones. They photographed every square inch of the room. Whenever one person finished snapping a picture, another person came up after and snapped a picture of the same thing. More people entered the room to take pictures of the group taking selfies. Another group filed in to take pictures of the people taking pictures of the group taking selfies, and still another group arrived and took pictures of all that. Then a very clever guy posted his picture of that frenzy, and the whole thing started up again because people remembered they had forgotten to post their pictures. So began an intricate process of filter selection and commenting and taking pictures of people selecting filters and commenting on the filters of the pictures they took. A woman took a picture of me. By now the room was full of people holding their phones aloft, capturing footage of all the other arms holding phones up high. It was a carnival of documentation.

Down below, people swam through a sea of knees to take pictures. They handed their phones to one another so people could take selfies with two phones at the same time. Their arms and legs were tangled, and it was difficult to tell whose phone was whose. They posed with one another, then swapped partners and posed and smiled again. They faced the camera. They made faces at the camera. They turned away from the camera. They twirled like spinning dervishes with the camera. Someone discovered the flash button on his phone, and it was deemed necessary to repeat this entire cycle with flash enabled.

More poured in. Soon the room was full. There was no more room to breathe, so this amorphous blob, this colony of lenses, exerted itself through the doorway and spread like blood out into the hallway. It splashed against the walls and ran like a torrent past the entrances. It swept away the placards and paintings from the walls and snapped pictures of them. They were ground up, and the glowing throng surged on.

Adrift in this sea, I fell forward and lost sight of the ceiling. My directions were mixed around. I didn't realize we were outside in the street until I heard the snarl of a bus rolling by. Some of the crowd broke off and swallowed the bus and some other cars. I was trapped in the larger portion that had now managed to photograph its insides. Every organ of every member of this hive was captured in high definition, tied together and streamed for the photographed eyes around the globe to see. We could even see their brains portrayed in wide angle and three dimensions. We took note of the heat signatures of their kidneys and looked over intimate x-rays. We approved of these images because there was no way not to approve of these images. Scientists were enlisted to develop a fifth camera to be attached to the back of the phone. Then all the pictures were moved from the phone to the cloud, where they could be stored forever. The copies left on the phones were deleted, then recovered mere seconds before they were permanently deleted. A picture of the excitement erupting from our photogenic mob went viral, and a whole new barrage of cameras from the media descended upon us. We smiled. All of us waved. We were very proud. A reporter from a local news channel asked me if I wanted to be interviewed. I hesitated to answer, worried I might look ridiculous or say something stupid. The reporter reassured me. "Come on, it's going to be on TV!"

I couldn't help but be convinced by this. Appearing before the world once it has demanded your presence is a duty none of us can deny. I tried to be smart and answer their questions thoughtfully. They asked me how I felt.

"Grateful," I said.

They took a lot more pictures of me after that. Before they could ask the next question, an image of me naked appeared on screen. People laughed. Then a picture of me in blackface appeared. People frowned. I was tossed out of the studio, back into the picture-taking parade as it swelled and traveled through the streets. I fell to the ground again. This time, my face sank into the concrete as feet tramped over my back. I plunged deep into the ground, crushed by the weight of the revelers above. I lived down here now. The lights of the flashes still reached me as the crowd took pictures of the back of my head. As I sank farther, it grew darker, and a light in my forehead turned on. It lit up the dark. I was finally alone, as if drifting in the interstellar medium. I could see, but inky blackness surrounded me. I began to shake. My face cracked, and just as my light was failing, I rolled over and saw Simone standing above me. The crowd of people in the gallery were all looking down at me, too. One of them was about to take a picture of me sprawled out on the ground when Simone made him put his phone away.

"Are you all right?" she asked. "You fell down. You're sweating, too." She smiled and wiped my forehead.

"I think so."

"Maybe you need something to eat?"

I nodded. She took my hand and helped me to my feet.

As we left the gallery, I put my hand on my left front pocket and noticed my phone was missing. Simone looked at me and said, "I don't know where I left mine either."

For once, knowing I'd lost my phone was a relief.

about the author

Born in Los Angeles, Michael Wilson studied literature and philosophy at Howard University and the New School. Today, he lives in rural California with his wife and three children.